Monster Moon

Curse at Zala Manor

BBH McChiller

STARGAZER
Publishing Company
"Educate, Enlighten, Entertain"

Published by Stargazer Publishing Company
PO Box 77002
Corona, CA 92877-0100
(800) 606-7895
(951) 898-4619
FAX: (951) 898-4633
Corporate e-mail: stargazer@stargazerpub.com
Orders e-mail: orders@stargazerpub.com
www.stargazerpub.com
www.monstermoonmysteries.com

CPSIA Section 103
Tracking Label for
Lead-free Compliance

Printer: Josten's Printing & Publishing
29625 Road 84
PO Box 991
Visalia, CA 93291

Run No.: E207780
Date: August, 2009

Cover illustration by Greg Martin
Graphic design by Michael Wheary

ISBN: 978-1-933277-10-3

LCCN: 2009933036

Publisher's Cataloging-in-Publication data

McChiller, BBH.
    Curse at Zala Manor / BBH McChiller.
    p. cm.
    Series: Monster moon.
    Summary : An ancient curse pits twelve-year-old AJ Zantony
    against evil monsters in a life-or-death graveyard showdown at
    midnight on Halloween
     ISBN 978-1-933277-10-3
[1. Monsters—Fiction. 2. Zombies—Fiction. 3. Vampires—Fiction. 4.
Horror tales.] I. Title. II. Series.

PZ7.M1293 Cur 2009
[Fic]-dc22   2009933036

Dedication

To my husband, George, who lassoed the moon for me!

L.K.

For Madeline, Jackson, and Julian. I hope you have many great adventures, and never be afraid of the monsters!

K.S.

For my husband, Joey, for pushing me out the front door to attend my first writing class. And for believing in me and in this project. And for Isabelle, Jane, and Grace. Don't let the bedbugs bite! And if they do, smack them with your shoe!

M. T.

Chapter 1

Oh, dragon crap! AJ Zantony groaned. He got that awful feeling something was about to happen. For AJ, every day was like Friday the 13th. If there was a pile of dog doo, he'd end up stepping in it. If he cruised past a cute girl on his skateboard, a tree root would trip him up. And if a major homework assignment was due, it mysteriously disappeared. But today was different. The feeling was stronger.

The school bell rang. The final bell of the day. AJ grabbed his backpack and zipped out the door. He heard the mean crowd heckling someone over by the flagpole. He slipped behind a school bus and hurried to the parking lot. Shivers wormed down his spine—his sixth sense had kicked into gear.

Beep. Beep.

AJ cringed.

Beep, beep, beep. His Aunt Zsofia honked the horn of her pink hearse as it rumbled over the speed bumps outside of Craggy Cove Middle School. The black coffin in the back of the hearse lurched from side to side as if a body was trying to get out.

"Hey, moanie, groanie, Zantony. Going to a funeral?" Calvin Crone, the sixth grade bully, yelled at AJ. Calvin nudged his cronies, Dirk and Runt. "Get a load of the witch at the wheel."

AJ turned his back to the bullies. He hoped Aunt Zsofia hadn't heard Calvin call her a witch. It would hurt her feelings. Aunt Zsofia was his favorite aunt, but he wouldn't be caught dead riding home in a hearse. Especially a pink one. And *not* three days before Halloween.

That morning Mom and Dad left on a last-minute business trip. Aunt Zsofia volunteered to pick him up after school and babysit him at her place. *Dang! I'm twelve years old. Why can't I stay home alone?*

Aunt Zsofia, his great-aunt on his dad's side, lived in Craggy Cove's creepiest mansion, Zala Manor. Thirteen generations of Zantonys had also lived there and when they died, they moved next door to the graveyard where they could stay close to home.

Stuck at Zala Manor for Halloween, AJ thought. *Just my luck.*

Every October, Aunt Zsofia threw a Halloween Ball, her annual fundraiser to preserve Zala Manor. She rented out costumes from her costume shop, decorated the mansion, and sold tickets for the biggest party ever held in their seaside village. Her pink hearse was the perfect rolling billboard. Today a sign on the hearse's door read: "The Monzsters Are Coming. Are You?"

Out of the corner of his eye, AJ spotted Calvin, Dirk, and Runt closing in on him. He wished he had the guts to stand up for himself or think of a good comeback. Instead, he wanted to get away from them, but not in the pink hearse.

If he ever needed his skateboard, it was now. He usually rode it to school, but this morning Dad had insisted that Aunt Zsofia pick him up. Mom and Dad promised to leave his skateboard and other stuff at Zala Manor on their way to the airport.

The hearse inched closer. "Yoo-hoo!" Aunt Zsofia called, pulling it up to the curb next to him, where the hearse backfired, shook, and died.

AJ didn't know which was worse, riding in a pink hearse or being picked on by the bullies.

"AJ-kins, get in! Get in!" Aunt Z said, flagging him down.

"Hahahahahahahahahahahaha! Did you hear that?" hooted Calvin, flashing his silver-capped teeth and slicking the sides of his blue, spiked mohawk.

"AJ-kins!" Dirk snorted as he slapped his knee. "Get in the Pepto-mobile."

"Loser-kins!" roared Runt, whose smashed-in nose made him look like a small bulldog. And he smelled worse than a sewer mutt, too.

3

"Oh, man," AJ mumbled under his breath, breaking into a sprint. He had to escape both the hearse and the bullies. *Hope Aunt Z understands.*

"Whasamatter, Loony Zantoony?" Calvin yelled, chasing after him.

The books in AJ's backpack banged against him. Something fell out. He spun around. A bottle. His latest batch of Monster Spray rolled towards the curb. His cheeks burned. He had to grab it before the bullies saw it. Too late. Calvin blocked it with his foot.

"What's this?" Calvin rolled the bottle in his hands. "Monster Spray?"

Dirk and Runt snickered.

"Looks like we got a wuss on our hands." Calvin bumped AJ with his chest.

AJ stumbled backwards, too shaky to fight.

"Scaredy Boney Zantony!" Runt shouted. "Your freaky aunt makes you part monster." He pointed at the pink hearse, its engine turning over as Aunt Z brought it back to life.

Calvin aimed the spray bottle and squirted AJ, shouting, "Die, monster, die!"

AJ wiped the spray from his face. It stung his eyes and smelled like pickled pigs' feet. *This is a rotten nightmare!*

Aunt Zsofia shook her fist out the hearse window as it crept along the street. "Zip it up, you hoodlums!"

"The old hag wants us to zip it up," Calvin mimicked, zipping his lips. "Is your widdle auntie going to fight the battle for baby-kins?"

"Yeah, and I bet she changes his doody diapers, too." Runt picked at a scab on his chin.

AJ wanted to disappear. Where's a hole to crawl into when you need one?

The new girl in class, Emily Peralta, brushed by him, pulling her backpack on wheels like she was on a mission to save the world.

"Look, it's the new ghoul." Calvin stuck his foot out to trip Emily.

She caught herself. "Nice try, Dingleberry."

"Monster mind!" Runt taunted. "Why don't you go back to Frankenstein's factory?"

"She's pretty scary-looking," Dirk jeered. "I think they screwed her head on backwards."

Calvin sprayed the Monster Spray at Emily. "Hey, this stuff doesn't work. Girly-ghoul is still here."

The bullies laughed, but Emily snatched the bottle from Calvin and tossed it to AJ. He caught it above his head and sprinted away. *Oh, great! Now they'll rag on me about being rescued by a girl!*

Footsteps pounded behind him. "Hey, skater dork, where's your board?"

When I'm a champion skateboarder, I'll show them. His heart beat faster as he raced down the sidewalk. Can't slow down, he told himself. At the end of the street, the footsteps faded, but AJ kept running.

A block later, he stopped to catch his breath and relieve the cramp in his side. When he straightened up, he faced the cliffside graveyard, overlooking the ocean. He'd run right past Zala Manor. A sea breeze cooled his clammy skin. With the bullies gone, he was starting to feel better.

In an archway over the cemetery gate, scrolled letters spelled out *Eternal Repose, Established 1692*. Beyond the entry, a whirlwind of fiery-colored leaves stirred, twisting around headstones and blowing his way.

"Spooky," he mumbled, a hollow feeling in his gut.

He backtracked to Aunt Zsofia's driveway but didn't see the pink hearse. She should have been home by now. *Where is she?*

At the end of her driveway, a towering gray mansion with purple shutters cast a monstrous shadow into the graveyard. Rooftop gargoyles glared down at him. The grotesque, carved stone figures were supposed to protect the mansion from any evil that might blow in from the sea, but AJ always felt as if they were waiting to gobble him up. As long as he could remember, Zala Manor gave him the willies. When he was six years old, he was slimed by a glop of slobber from a drooling gargoyle. At last year's Monster Ball, blood trickled from the gargoyles' stone claws.

He darted for the cover of the front porch. A hammock shaped like a spider web stretched between its wrought-iron rails. Only Aunt Zsofia would put that up, he thought. Floorboards creaked as he approached the door. He paused, never knowing what to expect next with Aunt Z. He tapped the door knocker and listened to its ding-dong chime. He rang the doorbell and flinched as it made a knock-knock noise.

When no one answered, he dropped his backpack and flopped into the spider-web hammock.

Crack! AJ jumped. It sounded like a cannon blast.

Chapter 2

Crack! The pink hearse roared up the cobblestone drive-way, backfiring and screeching. In the back of the hearse, the coffin bounced.

Aunt Zsofia hopped out, kicking the car door shut as her crinkly, maroon skirt blew in the wind. "I was going to report those hoodlums to the principal, but Mrs. Crowley flagged me down to buy tickets for the Halloween Ball. You know me, I can't afford to miss a sale. Sorry, AJ-kins."

"That's okay, Aunt Z."

Aunt Zsofia opened the back door of the hearse, pulled two grocery sacks out of the coffin, and handed one to AJ. "I'm expecting at least five hundred monsters at the Ball this year. Won't that be grand for Zala Manor?"

AJ pointed at the coffin. "That thing gives me the creeps."

She patted his head. "Sweetie, I get the Zantony coffin out of public storage each year. The Ball wouldn't be the same without it. It's a tradition. Everyone expects it." She grinned. "Don't worry. The coffin is empty. For now."

"Still freaks me out."

"It's all in fun," Aunt Zsofia said, fumbling with her keys as they headed to the front porch.

AJ read the carnival-style poster taped to the parlor window:

COME ONE, COME ALL

ZSOFIA'S

MAZSQUERADE

MONZSTER BALL

Halloween Night

8:00 p.m. – 1:00 a.m.

Tickets - $35 each

A black blur startled AJ. A scruffy rat crouched under the window ledge. He could have sworn it winked at him. *Nah.* The rat twitched its whiskers then scurried between buckled wooden planks under the hammock and disappeared.

AJ rubbed his eyes with the heel of his hand. He swung his pack over his shoulder, hesitating as the door creaked open. Inside was as quiet as a tomb. "I—I don't wanna go in," he mumbled.

Aunt Zsofia nudged him. "Sweet stuff, you've had a bad day. Don't let those bullies get you all riled up." She flipped on the lights.

AJ stopped. Zala Manor wasn't the same since Aunt Z's dog died. "I miss Thor."

Aunt Zsofia squeezed his shoulder. "I miss that old dog, too."

"Why did Mom and Dad have to go away Halloween weekend?"

"Business is business," Aunt Zsofia said. "To tell you the truth, I'm a bit disappointed they aren't coming to my party, but what can we do? The show must go on." She ruffled his hair. "Don't look so glum. You're in good hands with Auntie Z. Besides, your cousin Jasmyn is coming to the Ball."

Oh, great. He rolled his eyes. *Jaz is such a tag-a-long.*

Aunt Zsofia led him through the foyer and past the parlor, which she had converted into her costume shop, '*Ye Ol' Garb.*' They stepped through an ornately carved doorway into the ballroom. Massive stone fireplaces stood at each end of the room.

A lump swelled in AJ's throat. The last time he saw Thor alive, he was lying in front of a fireplace thumping his tail when AJ walked by.

Three stained-glass windows filtered the late afternoon sun into a rainbow of colors. Boxes of Halloween decorations were strewn across the room, but AJ focused on the shrunken heads, their lips sewn shut, hanging from wall sconces. He hoped they weren't real. Knowing Aunt Z, they could be.

Aunt Zsofia sank into the sofa and adjusted the gypsy scarf draped around her waist. "This is going to be the best party ever. I've got some new surprises this year," she said, "but I've got less than three days to pull it together. I'm so tickled Halloween falls on Saturday. A perfect night for a Monster Ball."

Monsters. None of AJ's friends were afraid of monsters. They didn't believe in them and hadn't for a long time. If they knew what he knew or could sense otherworldly creatures like he could, they would be afraid, too.

The gargoyles were a perfect example that otherworldly creatures did exist. Every Zantony knew it, even if they didn't like to talk about it. AJ's stomach flopped. "I feel sick. Can I go to my room now?"

"Of course, Pumpykins. I'll bring you some chicken soup to calm your tummy."

"Thanks, Aunt Zsofia."

At the bottom of the staircase, he looked up at the walls where generations of Zantony portraits stared back at him. Almost every one of his ancestors had a dimpled chin like his own. Their painted eyes seemed to follow his every move. He took a deep breath then darted up the stairs.

He found his beat-up suitcase and skateboard propped in the corner of the guest room, just as Mom and Dad had promised. He dumped his backpack on the bed and scratched his nose. The place smelled like lemon oil trying to cover musty odors. The drab, olive-green wallpaper curled at the edges like a swamp creature shedding its skin.

"Great." He kicked the bed. "No TV. No computer. No cell phone. No Thor."

Zala Manor was eerily quiet without Thor. AJ's heart felt empty. Thor was the closest he'd ever come to having a pet. *I wish he were here.*

Thump. His skateboard dropped and rolled slowly towards him. It stopped at the edge of a small braided rug next to the bed.

"Hmmm. Good idea." He hopped on his board and moved away from the rug. Skateboarding kept him from losing his mind.

AJ pressed his right foot on the back of the board, making the front go up. Perfect *ollie.* Then he jumped, did a *180* spin, landed in the middle, took a step backward, then a step forward so the front dipped and the back end went up. Next, a kick flip. *Wow.* Not bad.

"What's all that racket?" his aunt yelled from downstairs.

"Sorry, Aunt Z!"

"Why don't you do your homework," she hollered.

AJ dug in his backpack and grabbed his math book. "I hate math." He pitched himself backwards onto the bed, crossed his arms and stared at the water stains on the ceiling. They looked like ghosts circling a pirate ship.

Dinner arrived, but he only sipped half of his soup.

A daddy-long-legs bobbed along the window sill, dropped to the floor, and scuttled under the armoire. A bookcase, crammed with dusty books, butted up against the old armoire. AJ picked up a book with a skull and crossbones on its cracked spine. He swept the dust off its title. *Pirate Treasures of Craggy Cove.*

He settled on the floor and read about how pirates forced their prisoners to walk the plank, about how eating limes kept sailors from dying of scurvy, and how the hold of a ship was infested with rats.

Hours later, Aunt Zsofia waltzed in, carrying a plate of candy shaped like eyeballs with chocolate-brown irises. "Just want to keep an *eye* on you." She chuckled. "I'm serving these at the party. Want a sample?"

"No, thanks. Not very hungry."

She set the plate on the nightstand. "In case you get your appetite back. Sleep tight and don't let the bed bugs bite." She gave him a peck on the cheek and left the room.

"Bed bugs. Yuck." He checked the bed for bugs before plopping down with his book. The print blurred and looked like fleas jumping across the pages. His eyelids drooped. He yawned again and again until he finally fell asleep.

He dreamed of Calvin, Dirk, and Runt with silver thumb-tacks in their necks. No, they were silver push pins, and it made them look like Frankensteins. They chased AJ through the *Eternal Repose* cemetery and cornered him in front of the Zantony mausoleum. He reached for his Monster Spray and pulled out a feather. Wake up, wake up, he told himself, this isn't real.

He bolted upright. His heart raced. Recognizing the ugly wallpaper and the candy eyeballs on his nightstand, he remembered he was at Aunt Z's. Moonlight seeped into the room between the valance and gathered curtain top, its light making lacey patterns on the wall. Above his bed, an ordinary house spider hung from its web, casting a gargantuan shadow. The bells from the church tower beyond the graveyard tolled twelve times. Midnight.

AJ stretched the bedcovers to the bridge of his nose and listened. He heard faint singing and strained to hear the words.

"Three dead men on a pirate's quest.
Yeo-heave-ho and a bottle of rum.
Har-har-har!"

Shivers darted up AJ's spine. Where was the singing coming from? He listened harder. It seemed to come from inside the wall.

Chapter 3

The next morning AJ dressed for school. He slapped on a baseball cap and tromped down the back servant stairs to the kitchen.

"No hats at the table," Aunt Zsofia said, pulling it off. Behind her, the hooded figure carved on the basement door looked like a grim reaper biding his time.

AJ wondered if he should tell Aunt Z about the strange singing in the wall. Maybe it was just another weird dream. He drizzled syrup on his pancakes, took a few bites, and finally asked, "Aunt Z, did you hear singing last night?"

"No, Sweetums, I didn't hear anything," she answered, scribbling a to-do list for the Masquerade Ball on her marker board.

"I heard singing."

"Hmmmm," Aunt Z said, but he knew she wasn't paying attention. Sometimes she *was* clueless.

At school he hunched over his latest copy of *Monzter Madness* that he kept hidden in his desk. The magazine was loaded with monster facts. He flipped through it, searching for singing ghosts.

"AJ Zantony, are you listening?" barked Miss Riddle.

"Huh?" AJ slipped his magazine under his book and sat up straight.

"I've assigned science partners," Miss Riddle said. "AJ, you'll work with Emily."

"Oh, man," said AJ.

Dirk and Runt snickered.

"That's enough," said Miss Riddle. "Pair off with your partners. Because it's a half-day, you have only fifteen minutes to start planning your science projects."

AJ dragged himself over to Emily's lab table.

"I'm Emily," she said. "Emily Peralta."

"I know." AJ squirmed. "You're the new girl."

Emily chewed on her pencil eraser. "So, do you like science projects?"

"No. Do you?"

"Of course. I'm used to winning. When I was at my old school, I won the grand prize at the state science fair," she bragged. "And I also took first at the district's science talent search."

"Really?"

Emily clicked a small penlight attached to her belt loop. "I love science. It explains everything in the world."

He glanced over at his friends, Freddy and Michael. They stared back. Michael pretended to choke and gag. Freddy made fart noises with his hand stuffed in his armpit. AJ had hoped to be paired with one of his friends, but they didn't know much about science, either.

Since AJ was stuck with the new girl, he hoped she was as good as she claimed.

He looked back at her. "When do we start?"

"Right away," she chirped. "So, Zantony. What kind of name is that?"

"Huh? What do you mean?"

"Your background. Like, my mom is African-American and my dad is from Mexico. He's an archeologist. How about you? Is Zantony Italian?"

AJ muttered, "Zantony is Hungarian. My great-great-great-great-great-great-great...." He stopped. "How many greats is that?"

"I don't know. How many do you want?"

"Thirteen. My uncle, Bela Zantony, came to America from Hungary thirteen generations ago."

"Thirteen generations? That's so cool!"

"Maybe it's unlucky thirteen."

"Don't tell me you're superstitious."

He didn't answer.

"So...." She clicked her penlight on and off. "Why does everyone call you AJ?"

"I like it. So, what's our project?"

"What does AJ stand for? Like, what's your real name?"

AJ felt as if he was being interrogated by the police. She better not shine that light in my face, he thought.

Emily went on, "AJ could stand for a lot of things. It must stand for something."

"My name is Adam Joseph. I just like to be called AJ. Is that okay with you?"

"Well, I like Adam better. Adam, the beginning of mankind."

"AJ is fine, really." He lowered his head into his hands. "Oh, man." What had Miss Riddle done? She stuck him with a girl, a smart aleck, and a snoop. Three strikes, right off the bat. Just his luck. Emily was going to be a science partner right out of *Monzter Madness*—a total nightmare.

Chapter 4

During lunch, AJ passed up a game of basketball with Freddy and Michael. He sat on a bench far away from the others, chewing his peanut butter and banana sandwich and reading his magazine. He read articles about ghost hunters. Chains, bumps in the night, and even phantom screams, but no reports of singing ghosts—not even in the shower.

A hand reached over his shoulder and ripped the magazine from him.

"Hey, check it out," shouted Calvin, reading the cover. "Looks like Moanie Zantony is on a ghost hunt." Calvin chuckled and tossed the magazine to Dirk.

"Maybe he thinks he's a ghost buster," taunted Dirk, pitching it to Runt.

"Give it back," AJ said through clenched teeth.

"Ghost Boy wants his magazine back," razzed Runt, flinging the magazine to Dirk as AJ reached for it.

"What are you gonna do if we don't?" jeered Dirk as he shot it back to Calvin.

"Be careful," AJ said. "You're gonna tear it."

"Oh, we don't want to do that." Calvin ripped out a page. "Oops." He crumpled it into a ball and flung it at AJ.

"Knock it off, you chuckleheads." Emily appeared out of nowhere.

Calvin hurled the magazine toward Dirk. Emily jumped onto the bench and caught it.

"Looks like Ghost Boy has a bodyguard," sneered Calvin. "Come on, let's go dunk a few heads."

Runt snorted. The bullies laughed as they strutted toward the basketball court.

How embarrassing! AJ spun towards Emily. "I don't need your help."

"Don't get mad at me." Emily scowled and handed AJ his magazine. "I was just trying to be nice."

"Geez," was all AJ said, plopping onto the bench. Emily sat down next to him.

"What's their problem?" she asked.

"Leave me alone. I can handle them."

"Ignore them," Emily said. "They're just a bunch of brainless bananas."

"It's not just them," said AJ. "It's everything."

"Like what?" Emily leaned in.

AJ didn't answer. He wasn't about to spill his guts to the new girl.

"Come on. I can keep a secret," she said.

AJ wasn't convinced.

"Come on, tell me. What's bugging you?"

He hesitated then blurted it out. "First, my parents go out of town and make me stay with my Aunt Zsofia in her creepy house. Then she comes to pick me up from school in a hearse, a pink one. I can't sleep because I hear ghosts singing in my room. And to top it all off, Miss Riddle makes *you* my science partner."

"What's wrong with that?" Emily shrugged. "Anyway, what do you mean, there's a ghost singing in your room? Don't tell me you believe in ghosts?"

AJ looked away.

"You *do* believe in ghosts," she accused. "They aren't real, you know. There's no scientific proof that they exist."

"Yeah, well, maybe scientists have never been in a place like Zala Manor," said AJ. "It's the oldest house in Craggy Cove."

"Cool. What's it like inside?"

"Old and dark, mostly. Cold and drafty, too. Creepy. With lots of wood carvings everywhere. There's a hooded figure carved in the door leading to the basement. I hate the basement. No telling what's down there."

"Don't start that again. There's no such thing as ghosts."

"You wouldn't say that if you were there last night. I heard a singing ghost."

21

"Yeah, right." Emily clicked her penlight.

"Everyone thinks Zala Manor is haunted because of the cemetery next door."

"Wait a minute, are you talking about that old mansion at the end of Eerie Lane?"

"That's the one."

"I've been dying to see the inside of that house since we moved here. Hey, since we have to get together to plan our project, I vote we meet at your aunt's house. I'll text my mom and tell her we'll be studying after school. Who knows, maybe we can snoop around and find out what really made that singing noise you heard."

AJ wasn't thrilled about Emily coming home with him, but it wasn't a bad idea, either. He could get out of helping Aunt Zsofia decorate for the Ball and he wouldn't have to spend his afternoon alone in the house while she ran her errands.

After school, Emily met up with AJ. She jogged beside him as he sailed on his skateboard. She yakked away. He grunted in response.

"Hey, Ghost Boy." Calvin jumped from behind a hedge. "You got a girlfriend?"

"She can't be his girlfriend," said Dirk. "She's not a ghost."

"Maybe she's an evil scientist," said Calvin.

AJ glanced from Emily to Calvin. He wished she were a mad scientist, then she could pickle Calvin and put him into a specimen jar.

"Nah," said Runt. "She's not the evil scientist. She's the monster created by the evil scientist."

The bullies howled like a pack of wolves. Emily spun on her heels, eyes flaming and ponytail snapping. "Just because YOUR brains are dead doesn't mean everybody's a corpse."

"O-o-o-h," said Dirk and Runt.

Calvin smacked Dirk and Runt's heads. In seconds, the three of them were wrestling on the ground like dogs. AJ and Emily slipped away.

Aunt Z met them at the door to Zala Manor and showed them through her costume shop. She turned to Emily. "I hope you're coming to the Monster Ball, dear." Using both hands, she turned over a large hourglass filled with golden dust.

"I'll ask my mom. Cool hourglass." Emily looked up. "Cool chandelier. I love antiques."

"I do, too." Aunt Zsofia clasped her hands. "That's why I don't move to a smaller place. Can't give up my heirlooms. There are too many memories."

AJ wandered over to a suit of armor standing in the corner. "Is this new?" He ran his fingers along the seams of metal and over the swirls of embossed letters. The letters were so fancy he couldn't make out what they said. A tunic of chain mail hung inside it.

"Don't you love it? Got it off eBay. It's from a Hungarian castle." Behind Aunt Zsofia, a black cat clock meowed the time. One o'clock. "I've got work. No time for dawdling." Aunt Zsofia shooed them out of her shop.

They sidestepped boxes of decorations to get to Aunt Zsofia's library. Emily dropped her backpack and snooped around the room, reading the titles on the book spines. "This is like a museum," she said, as she zigzagged around pedestals, each holding an exotic animal.

"Wow!" she said. "An orangutan. A hyena. An armadillo." She checked out each one. "I wonder why your aunt keeps such a strange collection," she said, nose-to-nose with the armadillo.

"Who knows?" replied AJ. "Some people like stuffed animals."

"These aren't stuffed animals. They are taxidermy. Quite a different process altogether."

"Whatever." AJ turned the armadillo to face the bookshelves. "It's like they're watching me."

"They can't be watching you. They're dead."

"Not them, but maybe their ghosts are watching."

"I'll tell you again," said Emily, reaching out to touch the hyena's fangs. "There's no such thing as ghosts."

"Then why do I feel something watching me everywhere in this house? And I *did* hear singing last night."

Emily crossed the room to her backpack and pulled out her science notes. "We really need to get started. Whatever we decide for our project should be something no one else will think of. I want to win."

AJ sat down on his skateboard. "What about a volcano?"

"I made a volcano in third grade."

"How about electricity?"

"Fifth grade."

"Then let's hatch some chicken eggs."

"You got a chicken?"

AJ rocked his skateboard from side to side. "What's left?"

"Keep thinking." Emily paced the room, stopping again in front of the armadillo. "This is so cool!"

The hair on AJ's neck prickled. *I'm being watched.* An oil painting of a young boy with chalk-white skin hung above an antique curio cabinet. There was something strange about the boy's eyes. The dark circles. The sadness. Eyes as pale blue as his own.

AJ jumped up onto his board and scooted over to get a better look. "It's weird. I feel like I know him." He leaned back, then gasped. "Hey, did you see that? His eyes moved!" The skateboard shot out from under him.

Emily twirled around. "What eyes?" She took a step and tripped on the board, bumping the armadillo. It crashed to the floor. The armadillo's hinged tail sprang open, revealing an old, iron key.

Chapter 5

"AJ-kins! Where are you, my little Hungarian goulash?" Aunt Zsofia's sing-song voice floated from the ballroom into the library.

"Quick! She's coming," said AJ, scrambling over to the armadillo which was lying on its side like roadkill. He grabbed its stumpy legs and hefted it back onto its marble pedestal.

Emily removed the key and examined the hinged tail. It snapped shut. "There's a secret compartment inside its tail."

"Put that key back."

"No way." She slipped the key into her jeans pocket and straightened the armadillo. "Did you know that there are twenty different species of armadillo?"

"Good to know. Now put the key back."

"They're also endangered." She patted the animal's outer shell. "There...your aunt will never suspect we knocked it over."

"*We*? What do you mean we?"

Before Emily said another word, Aunt Zsofia poked her head into the room. "I changed my mind. I need some extra hands to help decorate," she said, tossing AJ a package of glow-in-the-dark spider webbing.

Emily intercepted it. "Got it!"

"No time for dilly-dallying." Aunt Zsofia's heels clicked across the worn plank floor. "Come along."

Emily giggled. "Dilly-dallying? Who talks like that?"

As AJ followed, he leapt into the air, trying to tap the door beam above him. Its strange, intricate carvings of angels and demons had always intrigued him. He almost hit the beam that time.

In the ballroom, Emily pulled and stretched at the spider webbing, sticking it wherever it clung. AJ placed paper-maché Jack-o-lanterns on the buffet tables.

"Put one on the harpsichord," Aunt Zsofia instructed.

AJ also propped black cats with hissing expressions near the gaping mouths of the massive fireplaces.

"Emily, dear, be generous with the webbing. We're going for that ultimate spooky effect." Aunt Zsofia fanned her ringed fingers. "Spider webbing is an art form. If you don't believe me, just ask any spider." She laughed as she centered a ladder beneath the candlelit chandelier. She lifted her hem and balanced herself on each step.

AJ steadied the ladder as his aunt hung furry bats with pointy fangs and red beady eyes. "Those bats sure look real," he said, half-expecting them to fly away.

"Nothing but the best for my guests," Aunt Zsofia said. "I have a reputation to uphold in this town.... Oops!" One of the bats flitted from her grasp and floated to the floor, landing near AJ's shoes. He picked it up by the tip of its wing and handed it back to her.

"Great flaming gas balls! It won't bite you. It's been dead for eons," she said. "I had these bats imported from Costa Rica. Aren't they marvelous?"

AJ blurted, "You mean those things *are* real?"

Aunt Zsofia tied the last bat to the light fixture. "Perfect," she said, admiring her work.

Emily stood beneath the middle stained-glass window. She lifted a globe from a lace-covered table. "Cool. Is this a real crystal ball?"

Aunt Zsofia wobbled as she hopped off the bottom step of the ladder. She scooped the crystal out of Emily's hands. "You wouldn't want to break that, dear. It's a family heirloom. Irreplaceable." She gazed through the orb as though she were in a trance. She batted her clumpy eyelashes. Her voice lowered. "Legend has it that a gypsy woman with magical powers entrusted this very crystal ball to a Zantony years ago."

Emily smirked. "Can you see my future?"

"Ahhh, yes...." Aunt Zsofia lightly scraped her long, blood-red fingernails over the crystal ball. "A troupe of monsters will arrive shortly. You will answer the door and escort them to the ballroom where I will be waiting."

Just then the doorbell rang.

"I don't believe this." Emily looked at AJ, her eyes widening. His feet felt glued to the rug. Aunt Zsofia nodded for them to answer the door.

On the front porch, they greeted a group of costumed characters: a bandage-wrapped mummy; a vampire with a widow's peak; a greenish, flat-topped monster; a wolfman in a shredded t-shirt; a creature with moss dripping from his arms; and a pale-faced woman dressed in a clingy black gown.

AJ and Emily stared at the ghouls.

"Vell, are you two mortals just going to gawk or are you going to invite us in?" The vampire flicked his black opera cape over his shoulder. "Ve have an appointment with a Miz Zsofia Zantony." He raised an eyebrow and flashed his pointy fangs.

In a deep voice that sounded like a man, the woman asked, "This is 1313 Eerie Lane, isn't it?"

"Y-yes," AJ spluttered. "My aunt is expecting you. Follow me."

Emily elbowed him. "I can't believe you just said that. You sounded like a butler in a hokey monster movie." She whispered excitedly, "These monsters are something else. I think I'm going to like this party."

AJ led the monster troupe into the ballroom where Aunt Zsofia was back on the ladder, pressing fake blood onto a large gilded mirror hanging above one of the fireplaces.

The vampire offered his hand. "Please, madam, allow me."

Aunt Zsofia giggled. "Oh, my," she said, as he helped her down. She nudged AJ and Emily. "Now make like good little ghosts and disappear while I rehearse the scripts with these monsters."

AJ and Emily slunk away to the library.

"Now what?" Emily said.

"Get back to our science project, I guess."

"Wait!" She pulled the iron key from her pocket.

"Now's a good time to put that back where you found it," AJ said.

"Aren't you curious?"

"If my aunt catches us with the key, she might…."

"Nah. She's way too busy decorating. Now, let's see…." Emily made a beeline for a drop-lid desk, but all of its drawers were already unlocked. Beneath the portrait of the sad-looking boy, she tested the key in a curio cabinet. She didn't need to. Its beveled glass doors opened easily. She walked across the rug toward a maple cabinet. "Bingo!" she said. "This one's locked."

"Better keep out," AJ warned. "That's where Aunt Z keeps her wine and sherry. Besides, the key is way too big for that keyhole."

Emily smacked the key against her palm. "Hmmm…." She stuffed it in her pocket.

"You've got to put it back," AJ insisted.

Emily flipped her eyelids up, exposing the spidery pink veins beneath them. Arms straight out in front of her, she

30

dragged her leg around the library like a zombie. "I'm coming to get you, AJ," she moaned, backing him into a corner.

"Stop it! I'm not kidding!" he said.

Emily held her sides and hooted. She sank into an overstuffed chair, flicking her penlight on and off. "You really *are* freaked out by monsters!"

AJ wished she would just shut up. Why hadn't she left that stupid light at home?

Emily pushed the ottoman to the bookcase and climbed up. She yanked a volume down and read the book's spine aloud. "*Werewolves. Fact or Fiction?* I say fiction. How about you?"

AJ didn't answer. He rattled through a collection of walking sticks kept in an umbrella holder. He plucked out the one with a silver handle. It looked like a dragon. No, maybe a sea monster.

"Don't tell me you believe in werewolves, too?" Emily tossed her head back and howled. "Awwrrooo...."

"Knock it off!" AJ snapped.

"Sorry, I couldn't resist." Holding onto the shelf by her fingertips, she shoved the book back into its spot. She tilted her head and read another title. "*The Raven* by Edgar Allan Poe." She reached for it. "Yikes!" Books toppled. Pages fluttered about her like hundreds of disturbed bats taking flight.

When the pages settled, AJ stared at the mess. "That's just great!"

Aunt Zsofia burst through the library with the troupe of monsters close behind. Gold and silver spangles slid down her slender arm as her hand flew to her mouth. "Great gypsy moon!" She lifted the hem of her skirt and tiptoed over the disaster. "You all right? You could have been hurt." She looked at AJ and Emily and shook her head. "Listen, you mischief-makers. Put these books back where they belong." With bracelets jangling, Aunt Zsofia slipped out of the room.

The monsters followed her, but the vampire lingered, swooping his cape across his face. His eyes narrowed. He laughed wickedly then glided out the door.

"Don't look so upset, AJ. At least your aunt never noticed the armadillo. Help me put these books back."

"No way." AJ grunted. "You made the mess. You clean it up." He hopped on his skateboard as Emily slid each volume back onto the shelf. He streamed towards the doorway. As he rolled under the beam, he jumped up and slapped his hand on the carved demon's face. "Got it!"

The walls rattled.

Emily gasped. "AJ, look!"

The bookshelf rumbled and broke away from the wall, revealing a wedge of darkness.

Chapter 6

"A secret passageway going up !" Emily exclaimed. "Let's check it out."

The narrow entryway was draped with cobwebs, sprinkled with tiny white puffs. AJ gulped. "Those are black widow eggs. And where there are eggs, there are spiders."

"Or worse," Emily said, "we might bump into your singing ghost." She snatched a cane from the umbrella holder in the library and swiped through the jagged curtain of cobwebs. "C'mon," she said, squeezing into the dark space and vanishing.

"Emily?" AJ whispered into the pitch-pirate black.

"Over here."

"Where?"

"Here. I found a staircase."

AJ waited for his aunt to burst into the room. She *must* have heard the wall rumble. When she didn't appear, he stepped sideways into the opening. "Why do I get the feeling that I'm not going to like this?"

Umpff! AJ tripped.

"Watch out," Emily said. "Sometimes stairs in old houses are uneven."

He stood still long enough for his eyes to adjust. Emily shined her penlight, revealing a cramped stairway. She crept upward. AJ felt his way along the rough brick wall until he caught up with her. She stood by an old plank door, hinged with iron straps.

AJ tugged at her sweatshirt. "Let's go. Aunt Zsofia might get worried."

"She has a million things to do," Emily reminded him. "Besides, we'll be back before she can say boo."

Reasoning with Emily was like trying to get through this brick wall, he thought. *Out of everyone in the class, why did I have to end up with* her *as my science partner, anyway?*

She squealed, "Omigosh! Something ran across my foot." She aimed her light down. A rat scampered along the wall.

"I think I just saw our science project," he said.

"Huh?" Emily asked.

"Never mind."

Emily jiggled the door handle. "It's locked. Wait. The key!" She fished in her pocket. "Betcha it fits."

"Look!" AJ said. "Nails." Four bent nails, two on each side, sealed the door like an old coffin nailed shut. "How are we going to get these out?"

"A minor technicality," Emily said. Using the tip of the iron key as a lever, she yanked at the rusty nails until they moved, then stuck the key into the hole. "See?"

"Yarrr…ye'll be sorry, swabbers!" a voice squawked.

Emily glanced at AJ. "Did you say something?"

Chapter 7

"I didn't say anything," AJ said.

Emily shrugged and turned the key. AJ sucked in his breath. The lock clicked. He hadn't expected it to work. "Aren't you afraid?" he asked.

"Nah," she said.

"I don't think we should go in there. It's locked for a reason."

"I'll wait here while you go get a permission slip from your aunt," Emily said, clicking her penlight on and off.

He paused.

She clicked.

"Well," he said, "maybe we'll just take a quick peek, but then we'll lock up and go back to our science project. Deal?"

"Deal. We won't hurt anything," Emily said. "We're just going to see what's in there. O-o-o-o-o-o! Maybe your singing ghost is behind the door."

Why did she have to remind him? he thought.

She went on, "My dad told me that a long time ago, ships wrecked near the cemetery and washed ashore east of the old Craggy Cove Church, where the rocks jut out and the waves break rough." She shined the light under her chin. "Maybe the dead sailors took up lodging in your aunt's attic." She laughed a ghoulish laugh.

She was making fun of him, wasn't she? He felt really stupid. "Okay, let's look," he said.

"Who knows, maybe we'll find something neat inside," Emily said.

"Like what?"

"Maybe a body. Or bones. O-o-o-o-o-o!"

AJ wished she'd stop. He also wished he had his Monster Spray, in case they stumbled upon something dreadful.

Emily pulled on the door handle, but it didn't budge. "Help me."

He cut in front of her and grabbed the handle and tugged. "This is really stuck. Let's forget it."

"Pull harder," Emily said. "One, two, three, pull."

Slowly, the wooden door scraped the warped planks of the floor and creaked on rusty hinges. They leaned back, their fingers grasping the door's edge as it grated open. The sealed-up chamber exhaled a vile breath. The door gave way, sending AJ and Emily sprawling onto the landing.

"AVAST!" a voice shouted.

"What's that?" AJ asked.

"Did it come from downstairs?"

AJ glanced down. A narrow box of light entered the staircase from the library. The sound couldn't have come from downstairs. It's coming from up here inside this room, he thought.

"AVAST! Landlubbing swabbers."

"What?" Emily turned to AJ.

"That wasn't me. It came from in there."

"No way." Emily looked around.

AJ was sure it wasn't the actors downstairs. "Maybe we'd better leave while we can."

"Not without a peek."

They peered in. Slanted ceiling rafters almost touched the floor on both sides of the room. Dusty junk lined the walls.

"This must be the attic," Emily said.

They coughed and gagged. Pinching his nose, AJ entered first. Emily followed. He checked inside the doorway. Just an old wooden rocking horse. AJ didn't see any ghosts or rotting sailor bones.

"Oh, wow. Look at all this stuff." Emily pushed aside sagging cobwebs as she squeezed beween stacked crates leaning against the rafters. She left shoeprints in the dust, alongside mouse tracks.

A lone window, its panes brown with grime and cobwebs, let in the only light. Dirt and bird droppings covered the window sill.

"Careful! There are mice and spiders and gross stuff up here." AJ coughed. "The smell is disgusting."

"Mice are DIS-gusting."

Watching where he stepped, he joined Emily, who snooped in every trunk she passed. After digging through each one, she wiped her hands on her jeans and grunted disappointment.

"See, there's nothing here. Let's go back down." AJ moved toward the door.

"Wait. Come look in these trunks. What if there's a treasure hidden here? I've seen on TV how people find strange things in their attics. A lucky find could sell for millions of dollars."

"But this isn't our attic."

"It's almost yours. Besides, you're living here right now. Like it's your attic for the weekend. Isn't it?"

"I gotta open that window or I'm gonna puke." AJ wrinkled his nose and covered his mouth as he ducked through the dust motes floating in the air.

"Breathe, AJ, breathe."

"I am breathing. That's the problem."

With pinched fingers, Emily lifted a faded quilt.

"Shh." AJ's ears perked. "Don't move. I heard scratching. There *are* rats up here."

"That's super DIS-gusting." She dropped the old quilt. "Eeeew! Rat poop."

AJ grimaced. "You don't make sense. You aren't scared of ghosts or monsters, but you're afraid of rats?"

"You would be too if you fell in a pit full of rats when you were five years old. Besides, rats are real. Ghosts and monsters aren't."

He shook droppings off the quilt and looked under it. An oil painting of a crusty-looking sea captain stared back at him.

"What if ghosts are real?" AJ took a corner of the quilt and swept cobwebs peppered with fly carcasses off the window. Then he wiped a window pane at his eye level and peered outside.

The old graveyard sprawled below them, lifeless except for clumps of sea grass growing near the low stone wall dividing the cemetery from Zala Manor. A wispy mist had blown in from the ocean. It wove its way around the headstones, like ghostly fingers dripping with seaweed. AJ could barely see the outline of a boarded-up caretaker's shack perched on the bluff overlooking the ocean. Beyond the graveyard, the lonely steeple of Craggy Cove's oldest church was a pale-gray shadow. Seagulls circled its spire and darted in and out of its bell tower.

AJ yanked on the window latch until it shifted. Then he pushed the old frame until it popped open. "Whew!" He stuck his head out of the window and inhaled the moist, salty air. "There's our family mausoleum." AJ pointed to a stone block structure with a flat roof in the cemetery. "That's where my ancestors are buried. My uncle, Bela Zantony, is in there." Then his eyes were drawn to the small mound in the graveyard, where he and Aunt Zsofia had secretly buried Thor. His eyes welled. Aunt Z had told him, 'This has to stay between you and me. It's illegal to bury him here. But Thor is family.'

Emily skirted over to look. "Wow, it *is* eerie out there."

"AVAST, ye scallywags!"

AJ turned to Emily. "What?"

"I said it's eerie out there."

"But, what did you say after that?" he asked.

"I didn't say anything else. Oh, maybe they're rehearsing downstairs."

"No. It was here." This time he felt certain.

"Maybe it's a remote-controlled microphone to scare away burglars," Emily said.

"Be serious. Someone else is in here besides us. I can feel it." Shivers wormed down his spine.

"Come out, come out, wherever you are," she sang to the tune of Pop-Goes-the-Weasel.

"I've had it." AJ was ready to leave her in the attic alone. He bolted for the door, but before he could pull it shut, he caught a movement near the ceiling.

"Emily," AJ whispered, pointing to the rafters.

A black blob in the corner rippled and grew.

Chapter 8

Webbed wings emerged from beneath the blob, stretching wider and wider.

Emily squinted, craning her neck upward. "What is it?"

"It's a bat!" AJ exclaimed, searching the rafters for more. Bats could be hanging anywhere. But there was only one.

An upside-down head with pointy ears and a snarling grin appeared below the spreading wings. As the bat slowly retracted its wings, its eyes flared scarlet red.

"Cool," Emily said, shining her light up. "As long as it stays put. Let me know if that thing moves." She poked her head into another barrel. "This kinda smells like molasses."

"Too bad the rest of this place stinks like an outhouse," AJ said. "Must be bat droppings."

"Avast and belay Ozor!" a voice ordered. On the wooden horse a black rat appeared, balancing on its hind legs and its long whip-like tail. The horse rocked. The rat's front legs thrashed the air.

"Huh?" AJ couldn't believe what he was seeing.

"Avast and belay Ozor!" The rat shook its tiny fist.

AJ stared at the rat's claw-like nails and long, yellow teeth. He grabbed Emily's elbow, jerked her out of the barrel, and pointed. "Get a load of that!"

The rat chittered wildly and waved its little hand towards the bat in the rafters.

In a flutter of dust, the bat stretched and flapped its webbed wings, then let go of the beam and plunged toward them. AJ ducked. Emily crouched next to him and covered her head. The bat circled the room, skimming past AJ's head, its wingtip clipping his hair. It swooped through the attic and soared out the open window.

"Scallywags! Now ye've done it!"

"What?" AJ asked, looking for the rat, but it was gone. He scanned the attic and spotted it near a knothole in the floorboards.

The rat squeaked madly, the hair on its back bristling. "Now ye've done it! Now ye've done it!" it ranted before it disappeared into the hole.

Emily stared at the spot where the rat had been.

"Did you hear that?" AJ said. "It talked."

"Rats don't talk," she said. "AJ, are you a ventriloquist? It's you, isn't it? You're throwing your voice."

AJ scratched his head. "It wasn't me."

"Yeah, right. Stop goofing around." Emily went back to snooping. "Look. A treasure chest."

AJ watched as she raised the lid of an old leather trunk. She really believed he was playing tricks on her. Hadn't she seen the rat talk? There was no question in his mind—the rat spoke. But how can that be?

Emily's eyes widened as she pulled out a frayed black cloth. It unfurled, revealing a graying skull and crossbones.

"It's a pirate flag," AJ said.

"This *is* a pirate chest." She rummaged through brass buckles, colorful scarves and velvet hats. "Who knows, there might be a treasure under all this stuff."

"Don't mess those up. They might be old Halloween costumes." AJ leaned over and watched as Emily unfolded a tattered vest with gold buttons. Beneath it, metal glinted. AJ knelt. He reached deep into the trunk and dragged out a sword and pistol. Cool, he thought. *Maybe there is a treasure in here.* He dug deeper and pulled out three feathers, one yellow, one red, and one blue. "Just parrot feathers."

"Maybe those came from a pirate's hat," Emily said.

Out of nowhere the black rat reappeared on the edge of the trunk. "Avast, scallywags. Those be mine." The rat leaped at the feathers. AJ jerked his hands away.

With its front claws, the rat grabbed the feathers, stroked them for a moment then put them in its mouth. The rat dropped to the floor and darted through a crack in the wall.

"Did he say those were his?" AJ asked.

"Who?" Emily said, her voice muffled from inside another trunk.

"The rat!"

"You're throwing your voice again. Knock it off."

AJ shrugged. *This isn't really happening.*

"AJ!" Aunt Zsofia called.

"We better get downstairs," he said.

"Wait. AJ, lookey here. At the bottom." Emily reached into the trunk and pulled out a small book bound in rough, cracked animal hide. She blew off the the layers of dust. "Achoo!"

AJ glanced at the book. Even upside down, he could read the word embossed on the cover. 'ZANTONY.' As Emily flipped it open, he saw handwritten, dated entries.

"It's a journal," he said.

"AJ!" Aunt Zsofia called again. "I need your help."

"We better go," AJ said. "We don't want Aunt Z to catch us snooping up here."

Emily hugged the journal. "Okay, but I'm taking this with us."

"Whatever." He'd agree to almost anything to get her out of the attic. She clutched the journal as he locked the door and pocketed the key. "Oh, no, I left the window open," he said after a moment.

"Don't freak. We'll close it later," Emily said.

"Let's go, then."

They headed down the stairs. AJ froze. "Shh. Listen. Do you hear that?"

"Three Dead Men on a Pirate's Quest,
Yeo-heave-ho, and a bottle of rum.
The first released, now beware the rest,
Yeo-heave-ho, and a bottle of rum."

Chapter 9

"That's it. That's it. That's the singing I heard last night," AJ said. "Sounds like it's coming from the attic."

Emily shined her penlight back at the old door. The singing stopped. She stood still, shifting her light toward the steps. "Sound travels in old houses. Maybe your aunt left the TV on."

"That would make sense if my aunt owned a television set. Nice try, though."

"There's an explanation. I know it." Emily stuffed the journal under her sweatshirt, then zipped up before squeezing through the secret passageway. They pushed the bookcase back into place then hurried through the library and entered the ballroom.

47

Aunt Zsofia glanced at them, doing a double take. "You look pale, like you've seen a ghost."

"I...er...we're, um...," stammered AJ.

"Probably low on nutrients," Emily jumped in. "Maybe we could use a snack."

"Moo juice," Aunt Zsofia offered. "How about some milk and cookies? That'll perk you up."

"Thanks, Aunt Z," AJ said.

As soon as Aunt Zsofia left the room, AJ whispered, "What in the world is going on here? I mean, come on, you heard the singing, didn't you?"

Emily bit her lip. "There must be a logical explanation. Do you think your aunt would play a trick on us?"

"No, she didn't know we'd be in the attic."

"Do you think she knows about that hidden stairway?" Emily asked.

"I don't know."

Aunt Zsofia brought in a pitcher of chocolate milk and a platter of pumpkin cookies. "When you're finished eating, do me a favor, AJ-kins. Please go down to the basement and get Mrs. Bones."

The basement. AJ gulped.

"Mrs. Bones?" Emily said, snapping a cookie in half.

"She's my life-sized skeleton. I got Mrs. Bones at a yard sale twenty-five years ago for a whopping five dollars." Aunt Zsofia rubbed her neck. "Why didn't I ask that nice vampire man to haul Mrs. Bones upstairs while he was here? He was so sweet to help unload the coffin. Oh, I suppose his devilish smile distracted me." She pointed to the casket. "The coffin and Mrs. Bones make a perfect photo op, don't you think?"

"Uh, sure, Aunt Z."

"Cool," Emily said, stuffing her sweatshirt pockets with cookies. "Where's the basement?"

Aunt Zsofia pointed to the kitchen. "In there. To the left."

Emily said, "Come on, let's go."

AJ hesitated, but he knew he had no choice.

He and Emily headed through the kitchen to the basement door with the spooky carving on it. Death's door. Emily opened it. "I'll go first," she said.

He peered down into the grim reaper's dungeon. The darkness filled him with dread. More creaky steps, more cobwebs.

Emily clicked on her little light as they descended the stairs. "This doesn't help much."

"I told you it was scary."

Suddenly, the basement light flashed on. "You silly nutheads," Aunt Zsofia called from the top of the stairs. "You forgot to flip the light switch." Her footsteps clicked away into the kitchen.

"Geez," AJ mumbled.

Emily sniffed the air. "P.U.! Mildew!" She zipped her sweatshirt all the way up to her neck. "It's cold and damp down here."

"What did you expect in a haunted basement?"

"Come on, AJ. Just because it's old and rickety doesn't mean it's haunted. Let's explore some of this stuff."

The lone bulb cast eerie shadows across the brick walls. The dirt floor was cluttered with junk.

Emily shuffled through piles of broken antique furniture. "Everything but the kitchen sink."

AJ pointed to the far corner. "There's a rusty sink over there."

"Look at this weather vane. Your aunt is a pack rat."

"Duh-h…."

Emily stepped over the weather vane. The Zantony journal fell from her sweatshirt and a loose page slipped out. She swooped them up and returned to the staircase, where she plopped onto the bottom step. She munched on the cookies she'd stashed in her pocket and shined her light on the yellowed piece of paper. "Cool, an old map of Craggy Cove."

AJ ignored her. Where could Mrs. Bones be? he wondered. That's what they were supposed to be searching for. He peeked behind a faded painting of an old castle, propped against a tattered couch. He called to Emily, "Can you check under the stairs?"

AJ picked up a fireplace poker and lifted the flaps of a dirty box. A hairy gray spider scuttled up his arm. He flailed until it plunked to the floor and scurried away. He looked at Emily. Her nose was still buried deep in the journal.

He covered his mouth and hacked. "If we don't get bit by a poisonous spider, I bet we get sick from breathing in all the dust down here."

"Listen. This was your Great-uncle Bela's journal. He did science experiments, and somewhere in *this* basement is his secret laboratory." Her eyes lit up. "A lab. A secret lab. That would be so cool to find."

AJ kicked an old rubber boot aside. "I just want to find Mrs. Bones, take her upstairs, and figure out our science experiment. And I'd appreciate a little help."

"That's the point. If we find Bela Zantony's lab, we might come up with a sensational project, one that would even rattle Albert Einstein's bones."

AJ scanned the basement. "I don't see a lab, let alone Mrs. Bones. And if we did find a lab, any experiments he left would be old and rotten by now."

"You don't know that," Emily said. She turned the page. "Wow! Bela won fifteen silver pieces-of-eight and a prized parrot in a card game. Sounds like he was more excited about winning the bird than the money. And get this." Emily read from the journal:

> *"July 7, 1698*
> *Three pirates are after me. They want the bird. They think the parrot knows where the treasure is buried, but it's too late. The bird is for my experiment, and tonight's the night."*

"Treasure!" AJ's heart jumped. "Does it say where?"

She flipped through the pages. "I don't see anything." She looked up and grinned. "Maybe it's in the lab."

"It's getting late. Let's hurry and find Mrs. Bones. Go ask my aunt if she remembers where she put her."

"Go ask her yourself. This is too good to put down."

AJ was halfway up the stairs when, through a gap between the steps, he spotted a skull with a rose clamped between its teeth. "There she is!" He darted down the steps, pushing past Emily. "I told you to look under the stairs. Can you put that down for a second and help me?"

Emily slammed the journal shut and slid it under the first step. She slugged over to AJ's side. "I bet there are a lot of treasures in this old house."

AJ lifted the skull and tugged. The skeleton was stuck. "Let's get these boxes out of the way." After they dug Mrs. Bones out, he said, "I'll take the head. You get the feet."

Emily picked up the ankles. AJ tucked the skull under his armpit, wrapped his left arm around the neck, then staggered up the steps.

"Poor, poor Mrs. Bones. I hope AJ's wearing deodorant." Emily snorted.

"Ha, ha," AJ said. "Very funny."

The bones jangled and shifted as they lugged the skeleton up two steps at a time. Its arms clanked along the banister.

"If we keep banging her around this way, Mrs. Bones is going to end up in a full body cast," Emily said with a crooked smile.

"Man, oh, man," AJ said. "She's slipping." He held onto the rib cage, while Emily untangled the ankles. "Ready?" They started up again. "Slow down," he huffed. "Geez, this dead weight is murder."

"Stop it." Emily giggled. "I'm going to drop her if I laugh any harder."

"What's going on?" Aunt Zsofia reappeared at the doorway at the top of the stairs.

"Nothin'," AJ said.

"Don't drop her." Aunt Zsofia helped them pull the skeleton up the last five steps. "Set Mrs. Bones against the wall. Where's her stand?"

"What stand?" Emily asked.

"The stand to hook her up on," Aunt Zsofia said, tightening the screw on the skeleton's head.

They returned to the basement. Emily said, "AJ, did you know it's against the law to have a real skeleton?"

"What?"

"Yep, it's true. Years ago it was legal for people to own them, but not anymore. I think Mrs. Bones deserves a proper burial."

"Emily, you're so out there."

"Let's hurry and get the stand. I want to find Bela's lab."

"We don't know if it still exists," AJ said.

"The stand?"

"No, the lab, genius."

After retrieving the stand and taking it to the ballroom, they returned to the basement to look for the secret lab. Emily snaked her way through mounds of castoffs. "I love this place. It's like exploring an archeological dig with my dad."

"Nothing down here looks like a lab," AJ said.

Crash! A lamp toppled.

"A rat!" Emily screamed. "There it goes. It ran straight through that hole in the bricks. Over there."

AJ stumbled over boxes. "It's the attic rat."

"How do you know it's the same rat?"

"It had a feather in its mouth," AJ said. "Let's follow it."

"Let's not. Rats are DIS-gusting."

"Give me your light." AJ crouched and shined the penlight through the hole in the bricks near the floor. "Hey, check this out."

"Is the rat gone?" she asked.

"I don't see it, but I see…."

"What?" she asked.

"I don't know. Maybe it's Bela's lab."

She dropped to her knees and joined him. They took turns peeking through the hole.

Emily smiled. "A secret tunnel."

Chapter 10

"I can't believe this house," Emily said. "It's full of se-crets."

"Move over. I can't see." AJ elbowed his way forward.

"You move over. It's my turn."

"Wait." AJ scooted back. "If we take out a few more of these bricks, we can both see."

"I'll get the fireplace poker." Emily jumped up and grabbed it. "Watch out so I don't hit you with this." She chipped the mortar around the hole. One by one the bricks fell. Holding the penlight between her teeth, she poked her head through the opening. A second later, she jerked her head out. "We have to go in," she said, clawing cobwebs off her face. "This must have been an old entryway that was sealed up."

AJ took the poker and jabbed at the wall until the opening was wide enough to crawl through on their bellies. They wiggled their way into the darkness. Slowly they rose.

Emily swept her light back and forth. "I can't see the end of the tunnel."

Dangling tree roots hung like snakes from an arched passageway. Crooked beams supported brick side walls. An uneven dirt floor led into blackness.

"There's the rat!" said AJ.

"Where?"

"I lost it." He strained his eyes. "Too dark in here."

"Well, good riddance!" Emily crept forward. "Look. There's a door. I'll bet it's the lab. We have to see if that's Bela's secret lab."

"But—I swear, that rat talks."

"You're being ridiculous. Rats don't talk."

"But—" He picked up a twisted root and tore through layers of cobwebs, slinging them aside. He edged down the sloping passageway, his hand slipping in and out of niches and alcoves and root-covered walls. They headed towards the door that could be Bela's lab.

"This air is so heavy and damp," she said, coughing.

"Yeah. It *is* getting hard to breathe."

"I think it's because we're deep underground. It's like descending into a pharaoh's tomb in Egypt's Valley of the Kings."

AJ scuffed along the uneven dirt. "You mean, you've been there?"

"Yes, with my parents. We travel all over the world on my dad's archeological digs."

"Man, you're lucky."

"Yeah, but sometimes I wish we'd stay in one place long enough for me to make real friends."

AJ didn't know what to say. He'd been stuck in Craggy Cove his whole life. Emily reached for the door and yanked its large iron ring. It didn't budge. He placed his hands next to hers on the ring and pulled.

"It must be locked," she said.

"Here. I'll try the armadillo key. Maybe it'll work for this lock, too." He tried the key. "It doesn't work."

Emily ran her hands along the doorframe. "There's got to be another key. I bet it's hidden around here. Check near the doorway."

"It'd be so easy if Bela had left a doormat." AJ felt the bottom of the door. "Nothing here."

Emily paused. "Maybe it's hidden in one of the other animals back in the library. Let's go see."

On their way back through the tunnel, Emily's light reflected on something in the corner near the opening in the bricks.

"What's that?" AJ asked.

The rat vaulted in front of them, cutting them off. Emily backed up, but AJ inched toward the opening they'd created in the bricks. As he neared the rat, it became more agitated.

"Watch out. It might have rabies." Emily's voice echoed through the passageway.

The rat glared at them as they crept by it.

Near the entrance of the tunnel, AJ stopped. "There's something over here in this alcove. Shine your light." He stooped down. "Whoa!" He jerked back, then grabbed Emily's light for a better look. "It's a skeleton…with a peg leg… and a gold tooth… and it's got a key around its neck." The key hung loosely on a rotten strip of leather.

"Did somebody die down here?" Emily asked.

"Maybe it's Mr. Bones."

"Avast! Avast!" the rat screaked.

"See. The rat did talk!" said AJ. "Now, you can't tell me you didn't hear that?"

"I heard squeaking," said Emily. "Probably your shoes." She reached through the skeleton's rib cage for the key. She almost had it in her grasp when the rat leaped at her. Emily screamed, snatching her hand away. "That rat attacked me. It *must* have rabies."

"Did it bite you?"

"No, it missed."

"Be gone, ye scurvy scum," the rat hissed.

"That rat means business," AJ said.

"Let the rat squawk. That could be the key to the secret lab. I'm not leaving without that key."

"I have an idea." AJ whispered into her ear.

Emily nodded, took a deep breath, and then stretched her arm toward the skeleton. When the rat rushed towards her, AJ plunged his fist between two of the skeleton's ribs and grabbed the key. The leather strap gave way. In midair, the rat pivoted and sprung at AJ, thumping against his chest and falling to the dirt.

"Got it." AJ grinned and waved the key above his head.

"Hurry. Let's see if it's the key to the lab," said Emily.

They raced back towards the locked door at the end of the passageway, the rat screeching and nipping at AJ's heels.

"That rat looks pretty upset," said AJ, watching its whipping tail disappear into the darkness.

"That's because we're invading its turf," Emily said.

AJ tried the key. "There's crud in the lock."

He jiggled the key harder. With a snick of the lock, the door opened. AJ took a whiff. "Smells like something died in there."

"All of the excellent labs smell," said Emily, trying to hold her breath. "Any scientist gets used to it."

"Watch your head," AJ warned as they ducked through a low doorframe and into a dark chamber. A large marble tomb dominated the center of the room.

"This isn't a lab. It's a crypt." Emily held her light close to the name plaque on the tomb. "It's blank. I wonder if there's a body inside."

"I'm not gonna open it to find out."

"I was so sure we had found your Uncle Bela's lab. Where is it, then?"

"How should I know?" he said. "Let's get out of here. I don't like hanging out with dead people."

She circled the room, patting the brick walls. "Maybe there's a secret passageway to the lab."

"Hey, genius, what if there is no lab? Maybe it was destroyed. Come on or I'm leaving without you."

"Hold on. The lab's got to be here somewhere," said Emily. "The journal said so."

A shadow crossed the wall. AJ jolted. "What was that?"

"What was what?"

"I thought I saw something move," he said.

"This is a crypt. Everyone's dead. Remember?"

"Emily, I *saw* something move."

"Probably that rat again."

"We need to leave. Now."

"Okay. It's getting late, but we're coming back."

AJ closed the door behind him. The key was still in the lock. He started to turn it, but Emily grabbed his wrist.

"Better leave it unlocked," she said. "It sticks."

"Okay." He pulled out the key and stuffed it in his pocket.

Halfway up the passageway, the scruffy rat reappeared, screeching wildly.

AJ kept his eye on the rat. "What's it trying to tell us?"

Emily gasped. "Look. The skeleton's gone!"

Chapter 11

"Where did that skeleton go?" Emily's voice rose higher.

"It's gotta be here." AJ shivered. The peg-legged skeleton with a gold tooth, draped in dusty cobwebs, had been sitting right inside the tunnel. Now it was gone. "How long were we inside that crypt?"

"I don't know." Emily scratched her head. "Long enough for someone to steal the skeleton."

"But who? Aunt Z couldn't crawl through that hole." He looked back and forth across the bricked-up archway. No skeleton. "This is crazy. It was sitting right there. You saw it."

Emily shined the light at AJ. "Maybe we're not alone," she said. "Do you think someone could've followed us?"

"No. My aunt lives alone."

Thud. Something plunked to the ground. Dirt rained on their heads. A rat clung to a tree root. AJ sprang away.

"AJ, I need your help," Aunt Zsofia called from the kitchen.

"Speaking of my aunt...." He poked his head through the hole and peered into the basement. "We'll be right up!" Ducking back into the tunnel, he said to Emily, "I can ask Aunt Z if she took Peg Leg."

"But the tunnel was sealed." Emily frowned. "She wouldn't know about the skeleton." She passed him her penlight. "Here, hang on to this." Emily crawled through the hole, leaving AJ alone in the tunnel.

He shined the light at the spot where the peg-legged skeleton had been. There was no clue. No drag marks, footprints or anything. He steeled his nerves and steadied himself against the wall. A skeleton couldn't just get up and walk away, could it?

Emily yelled from the other side of the brick wall, "AJ, are you coming?"

He scrambled to follow Emily but startled at an ear-splitting curse.

"Awk! Blast it! Now ye've dug yer own grave, ye spineless squid!"

AJ swung the light down the tunnel. The black rat perched on its haunches.

"Did ye hear me, swabber?" The rat drummed its nails on its teeth. "Now ye've really done it!"

AJ's jaw dropped. He inched backwards towards the tunnel opening, keeping an eye on the rat.

"AJ, hurry up, please." Aunt Zsofia's voice sounded far away.

On his belly, he wormed feet first into the basement. Emily was already halfway up the stairs, clutching the journal.

"We'll be right up, Ms. Zantony." She glanced at AJ, giving him a hurry-up look.

Inside the basement, he shined the light back into the tunnel for one last glimpse. The rat was gone. From the tunnel's dark recesses, he heard singing.

> *"Now the Second joins Count Ozor's Quest,*
> *Yeo-heave-ho, and a bottle of rum.*
> *Beware they meet at the Hall'ween Fest,*
> *Yeo-heave-ho, and a bottle of rum."*

AJ paused, biting his lip, then wobbled up the stairs. Back in the ballroom, he collapsed on the couch, kicking his skateboard aside, while Emily stuffed the Zantony journal under the sofa cushion. He spotted Mrs. Bones in the corner but didn't see any peg-legged skeleton anywhere in the room.

The coffin clunked as Aunt Zsofia dragged it across the floor. "Can you two help me stand this thing up?" she asked. "I want it against the graveyard backdrop." AJ and Emily leaped to their feet.

In the far corner of the ballroom, a canvas tarp hung from hooks high on the wall. A nighttime graveyard scene was painted on the tarp. The gravestone inscriptions read: 'I told you I was sick.' And 'Here lies Uncle Fred, we're glad he's dead.' And 'Here's dad, married to the woman on his right, shot by the wife on his left.' AJ noticed a change in the grave-yard scene from last year's Ball. The full moon had been re-painted blue. *That's odd. Why would Aunt Z paint it blue?*

He and Emily took one end of the coffin and Aunt Zsofia grabbed the other. They carried it to the corner and set it down in front of the graveyard scene.

"Now help me stand it up."

AJ and Emily steadied it as Aunt Z propped the coffin upright.

"All righty." Aunt Zsofia moved Mrs. Bones next to the coffin. "I've hired Olsen's Photography again. Last year the guests raved about their photos with Mrs. Bones. How do you like my blue moon? Isn't it grand?"

"What's a blue moon?" Emily asked.

What do you know? AJ thought. The know-it-all doesn't know it all. He turned to Aunt Z. "Does it really turn blue?"

"Oh, bats alive!" Aunt Zsofia laughed. "No, it doesn't really turn blue. That's what we call that rare occurrence when two full moons fall within the same calendar month. The sec-ond one is called the blue moon. And we are having one this Halloween. What a wonderful coincidence it happens the night of the Ball." Aunt Zsofia hummed and whirled in a wide circle before stopping in front of a wall sconce. She kissed the shrunken head hanging there and giggled.

Emily laughed. "Your aunt is a riot."

AJ picked up his skateboard and rolled toward the cof-fin.

"Why did we stand the coffin up?" Emily asked.

Aunt Zsofia grabbed her camera off the fireplace mantel and chuckled. "Step inside of it and let me take your picture."

Emily stood inside the coffin and stared without blinking. Then she folded her arms across her chest and shut her eyes. "If I die tomorrow, this is how I want to be put in my coffin. Only I want white roses on my lap."

Click. Click. Click. Aunt Z snapped away.

"My turn." AJ flipped his skateboard into his hands. "I'll show you how I want to be buried." He set his skateboard inside the coffin then balanced himself on it. "I'm going to skate my way into heaven."

"AJ-kins, your parents wouldn't bury you with a skateboard," Aunt Zsofia said, snapping more pictures.

"Well, aren't people buried with their most prized possessions? This skateboard is mine." He shifted his weight. *Someday, I'll be a champion boarder. I'll be famous.*

"My most prized possession is my dog, but I wouldn't want him to be buried with me," Emily said.

"What's your dog's name?" Aunt Zsofia asked, shuffling over to Mrs. Bones.

"Beaker." Emily flopped onto the couch.

"What an unusual name for a dog," Aunt Z said. "I love dogs. My beloved Thor lived to be thirteen. He died a few months ago."

AJ sighed. "Boy, I sure miss Thor."

Aunt Zsofia positioned Mrs. Bones directly under the blue moon. "Chop! Chop! On to happier thoughts," she said, slapping dust from her hands.

"Ms. Zantony, do you have any other skeletons or just that one?" Emily asked.

"Only Mrs. Bones. Why do you ask?"

"Just curious." She winked at AJ.

Aunt Zsofia draped a feather boa around Mrs. Bones' shoulders and straightened out her skull. "It's too hard to keep real skeletons these days because people may think you actually killed someone. But everyone in Craggy Cove knows Mrs. Bones. I've had her so long, she's like part of the family."

AJ and Emily exchanged glances. Is Emily thinking what I'm thinking? he wondered. Was someone murdered in Aunt Z's basement a long time ago and sealed behind a brick wall? Someone with a peg leg?

Chapter 12

As AJ stood inside the coffin, balancing on his board, he gazed up at the ballroom's stained-glass windows.

The first window showed an old white church against a green meadow. It sort of looked like the old Craggy Cove Church.

The second window showed three large gold keys against a bright blue background. Aunt Z had always called that one the Keys to Heaven.

And the third window showed a dark blue night sky with yellow stars and a full moon above a rocky hillside.

Outside the windows, a dark shadow flew past, startling AJ. His skateboard popped out. He slipped but caught himself by grabbing the sides of the rocking coffin.

"Careful," Aunt Zsofia said .

Snick! The sound came from inside the satin lining. He'd knocked something loose. Running his fingers along the spot where he'd heard the noise, he found a seam and slipped his hand through. His fingers bumped a knob. *A secret drawer. Who puts a secret drawer in a coffin?*

He glanced up. Emily was watching him.

Slipping his fingers into the secret drawer, he wiggled them around and felt a piece of rough paper. He pulled it through the lining and shoved the drawer shut with his hip. He glanced down. It was an old piece of parchment with scrawled writing. AJ stuffed the paper into his pocket and stepped out of the coffin. He picked up his skateboard.

What was written on the paper that had been hidden inside the secret drawer? He couldn't wait to find out.

Emily slipped up beside him. "What did you find?"

Aunt Zsofia looked over at them.

"Nothing," he said.

Aunt Zsofia's eyes widened. She screamed and pointed at the fireplace.

AJ and Emily spun around. A rat sat on the hearth. Oh, no! AJ thought. Not that rat again!

"Keep an eye on that thing!" screeched Aunt Zsofia, running towards the kitchen, her arms waving wildly above her head. "I'm getting a broom."

AJ stared at the rat.

The rat stared back. "The Zantonys be doomed," it said. "Ye shouldn't have disturbed the dead."

"What?" AJ ran over to the fireplace and knelt down. "What did you say?"

"AJ, what are you doing?" Emily yelled.

"Shhh," AJ said, then turned to the rat. "What are you talking about?"

"Take heed, scallywags. Ye've released Ozor's pirates. Their revenge is fierce. Beware All Hallow's Eve—the night of reckoning."

Aunt Zsofia rushed into the room, whacking the broom across the floor. "Out of here! Out of here!" she screamed. The rat darted between her heels and into the kitchen.

AJ followed it down the basement steps. On the bottom step, he called out, "I know you're down here. Where are you? Come out."

"Walk the plank, swabber."

AJ took a deep breath. "Who are you? Talk to me."

Silence. He started up the stairs but stopped when he heard singing. *The ghost!*

> *"The Third has risen to join Pirate Mates,*
> *Yeo-heave-ho, and a bottle of rum.*
> *Only Zantony blood can close the gates,*
> *Yeo-heave-ho, and a bottle of rum."*

The singing stopped.

At the top of the stairs, Emily asked, "Where's that rat?"

"I think it went through a hole in the wall." AJ continued up the steps.

Emily asked, "Hey. What did you find in the coffin?"

Chapter 13

"I didn't find anything in the coffin," AJ said.

"Don't lie." Emily huffed, clicking her penlight. "I saw you put something in your pocket. Tell me."

Aunt Zsofia called out, "Emily, dear, your ride's here."

Emily glanced down the stairs at AJ. "Tell me the truth, AJ." She put her hands on her hips.

Honk. Honk. Honk.

"Emileeeee!" Aunt Zsofia sang out.

"Coming!" Emily answered. "Well, are you going to show me?"

AJ shrugged.

She crossed her arms. "And here I thought you were my friend."

Friend? AJ thought to himself. He hadn't thought of them as any more than science partners. "Okay. Okay. You gotta go. I'll show you at school tomorrow."

Honk. Honk. Honk. Hon-n-n-k.

Emily fidgeted. "All right. See you in class."

After she left, AJ clomped up the basement stairs and stopped in the ballroom. While Aunt Zsofia jabbered with a pizza delivery guy at the front door, he wriggled the journal out from under the couch cushion. He stuffed the parchment he'd found in the coffin between the pages of the journal. Then he tucked the journal beneath his shirt before Aunt Z brought in the pizza.

"Pumpykins, how about a slice of monster-scab pizza? It's double cheesy." She handed him a paper plate and a napkin. "Pepperoni slices look a lot like scabs. Get it? Monster scabs?"

"Uh…I've got lots of homework. Can I eat in my room?"

"Go right ahead, dear." She pulled a stringy piece of pizza out of the box and placed it on his plate.

"Thanks, Aunt Z." He raced up the steps. In his room, he picked at the pepperoni as he read Bela's journal.

> *July 11, 1698*
> *The specimen's brain has been transferred into the head of a cellar rat. Only time will tell if the experiment is a success.*

"Wow! A brain transplant way back then. That's incredible."

July 17, 1698

Pirates returned. They threatened to dump me on a deserted island if I don't surrender the bird. Unfortunately, the parrot is dead, but its brain lives on in the rat. Plucked the parrot's colorful plumes. Shame to waste such exotic feathers.

AJ looked up. Hmmm…feathers. Could they be the feathers he'd found in the attic?

July 21, 1698

Pirates broke into the lab. The one with the mustache, who calls himself Count Ozor, drew his sword when he saw the bird's plucked plumage. Hunted me throughout Zala Manor. I tricked him into the attic, then locked him inside. The peg-legged one, the one they call Stumpy, put up a good fight, but the bulky buccaneer, Musky, turned skull-white when the rat spoke for the first time. "Shiver me timbers," was all he said before the pirate hit the deck with a thud.

The rat speaks! The rat speaks! The experiment is a success! My brilliant creation will be documented in prestigious European journals. Scholars around the world will clamor to my doorstep.

AJ book-marked the page with his thumb. Crazy. Uncle Bela was a mad scientist. He carefully turned the brittle page and continued reading.

> *Aug. 5, 1698*
> *Blast! Blast! Blast ! The rat won't speak pub-*
> *licly. My reputation as a scientist is ruined. I*
> *am the laughing stock of Craggy Cove. I may*
> *never leave Zala Manor again. Blast!*

Was madness hereditary? AJ wondered. He shook if off. "Nah. I don't even like science."

> *Aug. 7, 1698*
> *Ozor curses me. "Be warned, Zantony! I shall*
> *return in rare form, and when I do, your de-*
> *scendents will pay a deadly price." I must get*
> *to my lab and create a spell to protect the*
> *Zantony bloodline—before it's too late.*

"Oh man, this is getting way too freaky," AJ said, slapping the journal shut. A brain transplant. A talking rat. A pirate with a peg leg. *The peg-leg skeleton in the basement!* Could it possibly be Stumpy from the journal? AJ stretched out on top of the covers and set the journal on the nightstand. *Wow! A spell to protect the Zantonys. Awesome!*

He shut his eyes and his thoughts spun. He mumbled aloud, "What did this Count Ozor mean when he threatened to return in *rare* form?"

73

"Awk. A vampire bat." A voice pierced the quiet.

Am I dreaming? AJ thought.

"A vampire bat!" The haunting voice was bolder.

AJ peered over the side of the bed. Two beady eyes stared back at him. *Not you again*! The rat perched on its hind legs and jabbered.

"Slow down! Slow down! I don't speak rat," AJ said.

The rat paced the wood planks, whipping its thick tail about. "Who ye be calling a rat, ye scallywag?"

AJ shot back, "Hey, you don't have to get your feathers ruffled."

The wiry rat pounded its chest with its tiny fist. "Ye don't have to rub it in, mate. Oh, me beloved feathers."

"What? What did I say?" AJ leaned forward. "Wait. Did you say something about a bat? A vampire bat?"

The rat's nose twitched. "Aye! A vampire bat with teeth as sharp as a stone-polished sword. Ye are in grave danger, lad."

AJ clutched his neck with both hands. "Vampire? Danger?"

"*Grave* danger! And ye haven't much time."

The rat waddled across the floor, disappearing beneath the antique armoire.

"Read the clue! Read the clue!" its gritty voice sang out. "Or fer sure, ye be doomed to Davy Jones' Locker."

"Wait! Don't go!" AJ dove and slid across the floor. "What do you mean, danger?" He searched the small dark space beneath the armoire just as his aunt stepped into the room.

"What are you doing down there? Who on earth are you talking to?" She looked around. "I thought I heard voices in here."

AJ dusted himself off. "Um…I was practicing my ventriloquist act for the school talent show."

"Oh…." Aunt Zsofia kissed the top of his head. "Maybe I should hire you to entertain at next year's Ball."

AJ hesitated. "Sure," he said. *Great. Now how do I get out of that one?* He had a year to learn ventriloquism.

"G'night, Sweetums. Don't forget to turn out the light."

"I won't. Good night, Aunt Z." AJ waited till her footsteps faded. Would the rat reappear? He climbed back onto the bed. How could he sleep now?

Scrape. Scratching came from beneath the armoire.

AJ dropped on all fours and checked under it. "Hey, you're back. And you *are* real."

"The clue, mate. Read the clue," the rat urged, twisting its whiskers.

"What clue?"

"Ye found it in the Zantony coffin."

AJ had almost forgotten. He grabbed the journal off the table and pulled out the coffin parchment. He unfolded it.

The rat growled, "Now, yer listenin'."

AJ read the ancient handwriting.

> *Monsters on the loose,*
> *end of a bloodline,*
> *lest a male descendant*

vanquishes them
upon hallowed ground
in blue moon time,
from a triangle of Zantonys,
two times three feet deep,
a shining knight must slay
the avenging dead
by stroke of midnight,
lest more beasts rise,
thus Craggy Cove's demise.

"A riddle. It's a confusing riddle. What does this mean?" He looked up, but the rat was gone. "I don't get it. This doesn't make any sense. Monsters?" He winced. "Monsters on the loose?"

Chapter 14

AJ tossed and turned all night. Every monster that he'd ever read about in *Monzter Madness* visited him in his dreams. He woke up sweaty and exhausted but dragged himself to school.

After science class, Emily stuck out her hand. "Okay, where is it?"

"Hold on." AJ kept his skateboard under his arm and pulled the parchment riddle from his pocket.

As the class crowded out the door, someone stepped on his heel. "Move it, Ghost Boy." It was Calvin. Before AJ could shove the riddle back into his pocket, Calvin ripped it from his hands. "Well, well, well. What do we have here?" he taunted.

"Give that back to AJ," Emily demanded, as Calvin waved the paper high above his head.

"Hey, I bet it's a love note from Zantony. How precious!" He kissed the air. "Mwa…mwa…mwa…!"

"AJ and Emily sitting in a tree…," Runt chanted.

"Yeah…K-I-S-S-I-N-G," Dirk chimed in.

Calvin placed the paper with the riddle over his heart. "First comes love, then comes marriage…."

Emily huffed.

AJ's ears burned. "Knock it off!" He swiped at the creased paper. "Give it here or else...!"

Calvin shook the parchment in front of AJ's nose. "Or else what, AJ-kins? You gonna whip out your bottle of Monster Spray and spritz me? Ooooh…I'm shaking."

Dirk and Runt shook like a pair of skeletons rattling their bones. "Oh, we're sooooo scared."

"I'm melting…." Calvin flailed his arms and his knees buckled as he acted out the *Wizard of Oz* scene where Dorothy sploshes a bucket of water at the witch. "What a world. What a world. Who would think that a little dork like you could…."

Runt and Dirk leapt about like flying monkeys. Calvin waved the riddle back and forth.

Emily charged forward, snatching the parchment and stuffing it into her sweatshirt pocket.

Pretty gutsy move, challenging Calvin again, AJ thought.

Calvin spit a loogie onto the blacktop. "Aw, you two are a love match made in Loserville."

"Yeah, losers!" Runt and Dirk chided, forming an 'L' with their fingers across their foreheads.

Calvin jabbed at AJ. "This isn't over! You're dead meat, Zantony!" Calvin and his cronies strutted off. A second later, he wheeled around and pointed at Emily. "Your days are numbered, too, Peralta."

"Oh, stuff it!" Emily said.

AJ bucked his skateboard upward and tucked it under one arm, then swung his backpack over his shoulder. He turned to Emily, who was reading the parchment. "I think it's a riddle. Hope you're good at deciphering them. I'm not."

Emily read aloud. "*Monsters on the loose....*"

"Shhh, not here," AJ said. "Wait till we get to my aunt's."

On their way to Zala Manor, he filled her in on the strange journal entries he'd read last night.

"A brain transplant. How cool," Emily said, picking up the pace.

AJ knew that'd grab her attention. He could almost hear the wheels spinning in her mind. "Whoa!" He dropped his skateboard and jumped on.

A van was parked in Aunt Zsofia's driveway. *Good Riddance Exterminator Company* was painted on its side panel.

"Oh, no!" AJ yelped, barreling up the driveway. "They're going to kill it."

"Kill who?" Emily asked, following along.

AJ burst into the house. He hoped he wasn't too late. In the kitchen, Aunt Zsofia shook her broom and pointed toward the basement.

The exterminator tipped his dirty baseball cap. "Not to worry, ma'am. When we say good riddance, we mean good riddance. I guarantee you that." He clumped down the basement stairs.

"Can't have pesky varmints ruining my party," Aunt Zsofia said.

"You're not letting him use poison, are you?" AJ asked.

"Sure, why not?" Aunt Zsofia looked perplexed.

"You just can't," AJ blurted. "I mean, not right before your Halloween party."

"Yeah, some of your guests might be allergic to it," Emily said. "My grandmother once had a reaction to roach spray. She broke out in hives."

Emily *hates* rats, AJ thought. Why had she backed him up?

"Oh, dear, what in heavens was I thinking?" Aunt Zsofia ran halfway down the steps. "Yoo-hoo, Mr. Exterminator. I changed my mind. Just use traps, please."

"It's your call, lady." The exterminator lumbered back up the stairs. Within a short while he brought in twenty rat traps big enough to catch all the alley cats in Craggy Cove. He set them up in the basement.

"We'll be studying in the library," AJ told his aunt. "Then we'll check the traps in a bit to see if they worked."

"You're a darling, AJ-kins. I have so many other things to do."

As soon as Aunt Zsofia left the kitchen, AJ and Emily opened the broom closet where they found two Maglites, which were a lot bigger than Emily's dinky flashlight. They snuck back into the basement and using the fireplace poker, sprung each trap.

Snap! Snap! Snap!

AJ hoped Aunt Z was too busy with her party planning to hear the traps snap shut. "There," he said, "now the talking rat will be safe."

Emily rolled her eyes, then hunched under the staircase, springing another trap.

"Ahoy, thank ye, mates." The rat stood on a tattered sofa and pointed a feather at AJ.

He shined the light on the rat. "Hey there," he said.

"Awk. Ye helps me, eh?"

"Sure," AJ said. "I couldn't let you get caught in one of these things."

"Me thanks ye again, scallywags," the rat said. "Much obliged." It darted back through the hole in the bricked up archway.

"That's so annoying," said Emily, turning around. "Quit throwing your voice. But…I have to admit you are pretty good at it. You'll have to teach me how you do it."

"I told you, it wasn't me. That rat talks," AJ said. "Last night he told me to 'read the clue.' You know, the riddle."

Emily flicked her wrist. "Whatever."

"I'm not good at riddles," AJ said.

"I'll take a stab at it. I love riddles. They always have hidden meanings," Emily said. They sat down on the bottom step. She read aloud: *"Monsters on the loose. End of a*

bloodline, lest a male descendant vanquishes them...."
She scratched her head. "This looks like Bela Zantony's handwriting. It's the same as in the journal."

"Yeah, that's what I thought."

"This means it's the end of someone's family unless a male descendant saves them. I wonder if your Uncle Bela meant his own family. Very interesting," Emily said.

"Hold on," AJ said. "Are you saying I'm the male descendant who has to vanquish monsters?"

"That's what it says unless you can think of someone else."

"How about my dad?"

"I thought you said he was out of town."

"This has to be some kind of sick joke."

" I don't believe in monsters, but if there's a grain of *truth* to what your Uncle Bela wrote, your family is in deep trouble."

Grave danger, AJ thought. Just as the rat had warned.

Emily read the next two lines of the riddle. "*Upon hallowed ground in blue moon time.*"

"What's hallowed ground?" AJ asked.

"Most people consider burial grounds as hallowed ground," Emily said. "That must mean a cemetery. Maybe he's talking about the graveyard next door."

"Monsters on the loose...graveyard next door...blue moon time...." He smacked the side of his head. "Ding-dong. Aunt Z said there's going to be a blue moon on Halloween. Hurry, read the next line."

Emily read, "*From a triangle of Zantonys, two times three feet deep.*"

He shook his head. "This is complicated."

"We'll figure it out," Emily said, reading on. "*A shining knight must slay the avenging dead by stroke of midnight.*"

"Dragon crap!" AJ said. "A shining knight. Oh, yeah. There's a lot of them hanging around Zala Manor."

"Maybe the words are symbolic." Emily stood, stretched, and cracked her knuckles. "I don't have all the answers. Not yet."

"*Lest more beasts rise,*" AJ continued, "*thus Craggy Cove's demise.*" He knocked his head against the basement wall. "So if I don't save the day, monsters will come and destroy our whole town?"

"How well do you function under pressure?" Emily snickered.

"Be serious. What if this is real?"

Emily stifled a chuckle. "Okay. Okay. I'll try to be serious. Maybe there are more clues in the coffin."

"Nope, I checked it early this morning."

"Then I bet the answer is in your uncle's secret lab. I say we find the lab and search it for clues."

"Great idea, Sherlock."

"Why, thank you, Watson," Emily said. "That means we have to go back into the tunnel."

AJ took a deep breath. He stashed the journal in Emily's hiding place under the bottom step, then gripping the Maglite, he wriggled halfway through the hole in the bricks. He shined the light where the peg-legged skeleton had been. Still gone.

Emily followed AJ inside the tunnel. They twisted and turned through a dark jungle of tangling roots, searching every brick and timber, every niche and cranny, for a hidden entry to the secret lab.

Emily threw her arms up. "It's got to be here somewhere. The journal says so."

"Look." AJ pointed down the passageway. "The door to the crypt is open." He brushed past Emily toward the open door.

"I don't remember leaving it open. Do you?" Emily called after him.

Halfway down the tunnel, AJ tripped. "Ouch!" he shouted as his shoulder smashed into the wall, knocking the light out of his hand. He kicked a brick jutting from the wall just above the ground. "Uggggggh!" His foot throbbed. He grabbed it and leaned against a tangle of roots snaking their way down the bricks.

"Great going, Tinkerbell," Emily said.

Behind AJ, the wall gave way. He collapsed into a web of decaying roots. Branches scratched and clawed his face and arms as if they were alive. As he freed himself, roots snapped and popped like brittle bones.

"Oh, my gosh!" Emily screamed, looking over his head. "You did it, AJ! You must have kicked a trigger brick and found the entrance to the lab."

Chapter 15

AJ and Emily parted the rotting roots. Black beetles dropped onto their heads. They swatted at bugs crawling across their sleeves and up their necks. Emily gave her hair a shake. Before AJ knew it, she had ducked through the roots.

"See anything?" he called.

"Yes. An iron door!"

He crowded into the narrow space next to her. "Hey, an iron door with a big keyhole and no key to open it. What a surprise!"

"Let's try the keys from the armadillo and the peg-leg skeleton."

"Good idea." AJ tried the two rusty keys. Neither one worked. "Dang."

"Where there's a lock, there's got to be a key," Emily said, looking around, "but where did Bela stash it?"

"Anywhere, and it might take until Christmas to find it." AJ paused. "That'll be too late. Halloween is tomorrow."

Emily covered her head and disappeared back through the tangled roots.

"Where are you going?" AJ asked.

"Back to the crypt," Emily called over her shoulder. "That door is open. We might have missed something."

"No way. I'm not going back in that creepy room."

"It's no creepier than the rest of this place. Come on."

AJ gagged at the stench as they entered the small crypt. "Smells worse than before." He buried his mouth and nose in his shirt and peered about. His gaze fell on the lone tomb.

"Oh, my gosh, look," Emily said. "Somebody tried to get in the tomb. The lid's been moved."

AJ leaned over the partly opened marble casket and with his light peeked inside, half-expecting someone to leap up at him like in the movies. Instead, scraps of rotted clothing crawled with stink bugs and maggots. "Where's the body?" AJ's skin prickled.

"Looks like someone was laid to rest but is no longer resting," Emily said.

"This isn't a joke. Get a load of these drag marks." He pointed to the floor.

"Ew…a trail of maggots," Emily said. "Maybe some tomb robbers broke in, just like in Egypt, searching for hidden treasure."

His gaze skipped from the empty tomb to the drag marks, then to Emily. He gulped. "Not tomb robbers…the walking dead…a zombie."

"I don't believe it…but if zombies were real, they'd probably smell like this." Emily circled the tomb, running her hand its entire length.

"What are you doing?" AJ asked.

"Looking for a secret compartment."

"Let's get out of here before the zombie returns."

"Yeah, let's go before *whoever* opened the tomb comes back. Could be a hatchet murderer for all we know."

"Argghh…." A groan echoed from the other side of the door.

C-r-e-e-a-k! The crypt door slammed shut.

Chapter 16

"Omigosh!" Emily shrieked. "Someone locked us in!"

AJ shined his light into Emily's face. "Are you okay?"

"I—I think so."

"Is your heart pounding as hard as mine?" AJ asked as he pressed his ear against the door and listened. Nothing. He reached for the handle, but there wasn't one. *Of course, dead people don't need doorknobs.* He stumbled backwards, crashing into the tomb. "Emily." He gulped. "There's no handle on this side."

"We need help!" Emily pulled her cell phone out of her jeans pocket. "What's your aunt's number? Oh, shoot. No signal down here." She flipped her cell shut and put it away. "What do we do now?" she asked.

"I don't know," AJ mumbled. He wanted to shout for help, but he knew his aunt wouldn't hear them.

"We *have* to do something. No one knows we're down here."

"You're wrong. The zombie knows we're here."

"There's no such thing as zombies," Emily said.

"Arrgghh." There it was again. A ferocious growl. And a putrid stench. The handle on the other side of the ancient door rattled.

"Smells like a zombie," AJ said. Shivers coiled down his spine.

"How do you know what a zombie smells like?" Emily asked.

"I don't know how I know. But I just know." How could he explain the Zantony sixth sense?

They crouched behind the tomb and flipped off their lights. *What if it comes back in?*

AJ held his breath. They sat in total darkness. His fingers clenched the cold marble of the tomb. AJ's skin felt like it was crawling with maggots, but he didn't dare move. Eventually both the smell and the sound of dragging faded away.

"I think it's gone," he whispered.

"Who could it be?" Emily's voice trembled. "If these tunnels lead outside, then any tomb robber could be down here searching for treasure. And maybe they don't want us in the way." She clicked her light back on. The beam bounced from wall to wall around the crypt. "We're sealed in," she said.

"And deep underground."

Emily gasped. "Buried alive!"

"No!" AJ swept his light upwards. "There's gotta be a way out." The beam skimmed the wall, across the sconces on either side of the door, past the plaque with no name, and settled on a brick sticking out of the wall high up near the ceiling. *Maybe another trigger brick. Could luck strike twice?*

"Stand back. I'm going to try something." He handed Emily his Maglite. "Up there. Shine it up there." AJ hoisted himself up onto the lid of the tomb and slowly stood. He had to be careful not to fall inside the open part. The lid wobbled as he stretched for the brick. His fingers fell short. "Oh, crap!" He had to try again. "Hold the light steady." He pointed to a thick, twisted root that hung above him. Could it hold his weight?

"What are you doing?"

"That brick, I need to reach it. It could be our way out."

Emily's light zoomed in on the brick and then back to the thick root. "AJ Zantony, you're brilliant. Go for it."

He jumped and grabbed at the root but missed and dropped to the ground. He climbed back up on the tomb and took a deep breath. "I'm going to try again." He leaped and grabbed the root.

"Good going," Emily said.

AJ hung in midair and rocked to build momentum. His arms throbbed. He swung over the open tomb. With each pass, his feet got closer to the brick.

"Kick it!" she yelled. "Kick it!"

On his next swing, mustering all his strength, he drew back his knee, then side-kicked the brick. It was too dark to tell if it moved.

"You got it!" she shouted.

His palms burned and he lost his grip and fell.

They waited. It seemed like forever. Nothing happened. AJ felt he'd let Emily down.

She lowered her light. "We'll die down here," she whispered in the dark.

"No, we won't." Circling the tomb, he cursed and kicked the crypt walls. He tasted dirty sweat and spit it out. Stopping at the head of the tomb, he felt like a volcano ready to explode. "We are *not* going to die!" He nailed the wall with a fierce kick.

The wall *g-r-r-r-o-a-n-e-d.*

Emily jerked her light toward it. "It's opening! It's opening!"

There was just enough space for them to squirm through, if they held their breaths and sucked in their stomachs. "Let's try it," he said. "We have nothing to lose."

"I hope this is a way out." Emily squeezed sideways into the dark space as it started to sandwich shut.

"Hurry!" AJ pushed her and lunged through the narrow passageway just as the wall sucked closed and sealed behind them. They stood cramped together in a narrow earthen shaft. The air hung heavy. It was hard to breathe.

"This is worse than the crypt!" Emily said. "Now we're really buried alive!"

"Where are we?" AJ shuddered.

"Y-e-o-w!" Emily shrieked, her head jerking back. "My hair is caught."

AJ peeked over her shoulder. "Oh, dragon crap!"

Chapter 17

"Wh-what? What is it?" Emily stammered.

"A skeleton…."

"Get it off!" she screeched, thrashing her arms and shaking her head.

"Hold still!" He separated her ponytail from long, bony fingers sticking out of the cracked dirt wall.

"Ouch!" She spun around, panting.

Strands of her hair still clung in the grip of a skeletal hand. A gold ring emblazoned with a large 'Z' adorned one of its fingers.

"Oh, my gosh. The Zantony ring. Must be one of my dead relatives."

"That means…," Emily said.

AJ gulped. "We're under the graveyard."

Emily pointed her flashlight. "Look, stairs!" The beam wobbled along crooked steps curling upward.

"Maybe it will lead us out," AJ said. He braced himself against the wall as he crept up narrow steps cut into the earth. Emily followed close behind.

His footing slipped. Dirt crumbled and gave way. "Careful. The ground is breaking apart." He stopped abruptly. "Oh, crud! Dead end."

"You're kidding." She clung to the back of his shirt.

"I wish I were kidding. The steps end here."

"Oh, great," she grumbled. "You and your aunt's weird house are going to get us killed!"

"We wouldn't be in this mess if you hadn't insisted on searching for that stupid lab."

"Don't forget, you're the one who wanted to hunt for treasure."

"I can't believe you're dumping this on me!" AJ huffed, waving his Maglite. It clanged overhead. Dirt rained down. He squeezed his eyes shut, expecting a cave-in. Emily grabbed his waist. They coughed and choked.

Slowly, the shower of dirt stopped.

"What was that sound? I thought I heard metal," Emily said. "Look! What's that?"

AJ shined his light upward. The waffle pattern of an old iron grate, caked with grime, was visible in the dirt ceiling. He stood on his tiptoes. "Might be a way out. Help me loosen it."

Using their Maglites together, they pushed the grate upward and it gave way, screeching as it slid open.

"That was way too easy," Emily said. "Wonder where it goes?"

AJ grabbed a rock jutting from the dirt wall and using it as a handhold, scaled upwards and hoisted himself out. It was like the time he went rock climbing with Uncle Harrison and cousin Jaz. He lay on his stomach and reached down to pull Emily up. But she climbed out on her own. They replaced the grate and looked around.

They stood in a dark chamber lined with marble vaults, engraved with one Zantony name after another, their bones entombed in the walls. "We must be inside my family's mausoleum," AJ said.

"So there's gotta be a way out."

They shuffled past a stone monument depicting the Zantony coat-of-arms, just like the one that hung above the fireplace in his father's study. Carved on the medieval shield were the head of a howling wolf, a castle, crossed swords, and the all-seeing eye, the same eye that seemed to follow him wherever he went.

"There's the door!" Emily dashed toward it. "Please. Please. Please don't be locked." She pushed. It scraped open.

They darted out into the *Eternal Repose* cemetery and sucked in the fresh air. AJ kissed a cherub on a moss-covered headstone. They laughed hysterically, collapsing onto a clump of grass.

"Wow! That was a close call," Emily said.

"Yeah, too close," AJ agreed. "Someone doesn't want us snooping around down there."

Emily picked at clumps of sea grass. "The journal mentions a treasure. Maybe that's what this is all about. But who else would know about it?"

"Whoever locked us in, that's who."

"This is starting to creep me out." Emily paused. "We really could have died in there."

"Yeah, I know," AJ said. "Then *we'd* be zombies!" He sat on a gravestone. "But we didn't die. We made it out and we're not zombies."

Emily stood and giggled nervously. "That's right. We're zomBUDDIES!"

"Yeah. Zombuds. I like that. We smell like it, too."

Emily dusted off her jeans. "Yeah, like we just crawled out of a grave."

"We did." He raked his fingers through his gritty hair. A beetle fell to the ground.

"Ick," she said. "Let's get back to your aunt's."

"Aunt Z has a gazebo in her backyard. We can talk there."

"Let's take Bela's journal and the map. We need to study them if we want to learn about the lab."

"And the treasure," AJ said. "But we can't let Aunt Z see us like this. She'll ask too many questions."

"Shouldn't we tell her and have her call the police?"

"No, not right before her party. If word got out, who'd come? Besides, what could we tell the police? No one would believe us, anyway."

AJ tiptoed inside the kitchen door, dashed past the grim reaper carving and down the basement stairs, where he retrieved the journal and map. He met Emily in the kitchen. They grabbed sodas from the fridge and hurried outside to the gazebo.

He set the map on the picnic table and opened the journal. It flopped open to a page with a handwritten letter stuck to it. "What's this?" he asked.

A wax seal with the initials "C.O." stamped on it held the old letter to the page.

"Open it," Emily said.

He read the letter:

> *"Treasure's claim*
> *belongs to three*
> *dead or alive*
> *so shall it be.*
> *Cursed be the one*
> *who won the bird.*
> *T'ain't last of us*
> *that he has heard.*
> *He can't escape*
> *us in his lab,*
> *nor in the dark,*
> *nor under slabs.*
> *His blood we'll spill*
> *and all his kin*
> *till the treasure*
> *is ours again."*

"Whoa!" AJ pointed to a journal entry beneath the letter. He read: *"Received letter from Count Ozor today putting a curse on me and mine. I swear to undo it and put an end to his evil."*

"Omigosh! The 'C.O.' stamped in wax must stand for Count Ozor," Emily said.

"Uh-oh. Looks like this Count Ozor was out for blood," AJ said. "And it sounds like he was threatening my family." He jumped up, bumping the journal off the table and knocking over his drink.

Emily dove for the journal, landing with a thud on the gazebo floor. "Got it!" As she lifted it up, an odd-looking skeleton key slipped out of the book's spine and fell between the floorboards.

"Awk! Ye clumsy scallywags!"

AJ plopped down and peered through the cracks between the planks.

Underneath him, a rat rubbed its head and returned AJ's stare. "What ye be lookin' at?" it grumbled.

It's the rat. The talking rat from my bedroom.

"Ummm," AJ muttered. "The key. I need that key."

Behind him, he heard Emily. "Get it, AJ. It might be the key to the lab!"

The space under the gazebo wasn't large enough for AJ to crawl through and his hand didn't fit between the floorboards either. "Great. Now what?"

The rat spoke, "Ye might try the magic word, matey."

"Huh...? Do you mean 'please'?"

In an instant, the rat appeared on the gazebo steps with the key in its mouth. He spit it out at AJ's feet. "Here. Ye lads might be needing this."

"Believe me now?" AJ said.

Emily stared, glassy-eyed. "Oh, my gosh!" she muttered. "It *does* talk! B-but there's got to be an explanation...."

AJ picked the key up and dangled it in front of her nose.

"Do you think it's the key to the lab?" Emily asked AJ.

Chapter 18

The rat thumped the planks of the gazebo with its tail. "Aye, mateys, ye had the key to Bela's lab under yer sniffers all this time."

"Is the iron door, the one hidden behind the tree roots, the entry to the lab?" Emily looked down at the rat. "I can't believe I'm talking to a rodent."

The rat twittered at Emily. "Aye, matey. Bela hid the key to his lab in the spine of his book of private thoughts. Saw him with me own eyes the day he hid the journal in the attic."

"How can you know that?" AJ asked.

"I already told ye. I was there."

"You couldn't have been there," Emily said. "That was more than 300 years ago."

"Assuming you were there, why didn't you tell me about the key?"

The rat squawked, "Ye didn't ask, mate. Besides, I wasn't sure ye were trustworthy."

"You can trust us," said AJ.

"After ye saved me from them deadly traps today, I be forever indebted." The rat stood on his haunches. With one paw placed on its belly and the other behind its back, it bowed. "Vlad, at yer service."

"Vlad?" AJ asked, "Is that your name?"

"Aye! And mighty proud of it."

Emily half-smiled. "Even though I hate rats," she muttered, looking at Vlad. "Nothing personal, but—"

Vlad parroted, "Nothing personal. Nothing personal. Awk!"

"—the thought of you caught in one of those rat traps... seems cruel," Emily said.

"Speaking of traps," AJ cut in, "the journal said Bela trapped Count Ozor in the attic. Did he?"

"Aye! Bela put a curse on the count and locked him up for all eternity. Then you nosy lads come along and released Ozor and his two rotten henchmen."

"We did?" AJ asked.

"Aye! I warned ye over and over. Them dead pirates be *monsters* now. Out for revenge!"

"Huh?"

"Aye, matey, monsters on the loose." Vlad sat back on his haunches and belted out:

> *"Ye caused things to go from bad to worse,*
> *Yeo-heave-ho, and a bottle of rum.*
> *Now a Zantony must lift the curse,*
> *Yeo-heave-ho, and a bottle of rum."*

"Oh my gosh!" AJ said. "*You're* the singing ghost in the walls. But you're not a ghost."

"Aye. Got me voice from me sweet mum."

"See," Emily gloated. "There's no such thing as ghosts. I told you there's an explanation for everything."

Ignoring Emily, AJ asked, "So you mean Ozor's henchmen…?"

"Awk! Traitors they be. It's in Bela's journal."

"You mean the pirates Stumpy and Musky are Ozor's henchmen?" AJ remembered reading about them in the journal.

"Aye, mateys, their remains be the peg-leg skeleton ye found in the tunnel and a zombie…."

AJ glanced at Emily. "Did you hear that? That explains the stench in the crypt."

"Aye, that be Musky." The hair along Vlad's spine bristled like a scrub brush. "Aye. Scurvy bilge rats! Stumpy and Musky kidnapped me when I was a spry young parrot. They threw me feathered self into a burlap bag, then lost me in a game of dice while the captain of the *Golden Tortuga* caught a few winks. Ozor had a fit when he found out what those two drunken fools had done. Ozor knew I held the secret to the Captain's treasure."

"That's a fascinating story." Emily gathered the journal and the map. "But I'm dying to see the inside of Bela's lab. Let's go."

"Is that where the treasure is hidden?" AJ asked.

Vlad puffed up his chest. "I'll never tell. I'll never tell."

"Come on," Emily urged, hurrying down the gazebo steps and heading toward Zala Manor's back door. "I can't wait to see Bela's lab."

"Okay, but we better be careful down there. We don't want to be locked in another tomb," AJ said. "Might not be so lucky next time."

"Let's keep a lookout for hidden passages. There has to be another way tomb robbers could find their way in here," Emily said.

They raced to the basement, wriggled through the hole in the bricks, and burst into the tunnel. The rat paced in front of the curtain of rotting tree roots.

AJ glanced up and down the passageway before he and Emily pushed their way through the roots to the iron door.

Panting, Emily tapped her foot and held out her hand. "Fork over the key."

"No." He turned to Vlad. "I was wondering—how *did* we release Ozor and his henchmen?"

Vlad said, "Ye opened the attic window, mate."

AJ slipped the key into the door's lock.

"Remember, AJ?" Emily said. "You did open the window in the attic and that bat flew out."

"Aye. That be the count."

"But it doesn't make sense," AJ said. "I mean, why would Bela hide his journal in the attic if opening the door risked releasing Count Ozor?"

While AJ worked the lock, Vlad sharpened his claws with his front teeth. "Bela believed Ozor had expired, so thinking it was safe, he unlocked the attic door…." The rat stopped and admired his razor-ripping nails.

"And?" AJ said.

Vlad looked up. "And what?"

"Ozor. Was he dead?" AJ asked.

"More like…the walking undead. Ozor be bit by a vampire bat in the old country. Bela wanted to hide the journal in the attic where no one would ever find it. Luck be on Bela's side. He entered during the day while Ozor slept."

"That's right,"AJ said, snapping his fingers. "Vampires usually sleep during the day and stalk their victims at night." He'd read about vampires in *Monzter Madness*. "So, you're saying that after Bela hid his journal, he nailed the attic door shut and it hasn't been opened since?"

The rat scratched the dirt floor. "Aye! Unknowingly, Bela left his journal in the hands of Ozor. Fortunately, Bela's curse kept Ozor sealed in the attic. Only a Zantony possessed the power to free him." Vlad stood on his haunches with his paws on his hips and glared at AJ.

"What?" AJ threw his arms in the air. "How was I supposed to know there was a vampire in the attic waiting to be released?"

"Vampires are a myth," Emily said.

"You're wrong!" AJ jiggled the lock and straightened up at the sound of the click. "And I suppose rats don't speak, either."

"Well, there's got to be a logical explanation for that, too. I'm sure of it."

The door creaked open.

"This *is* Bela's laboratory," AJ said. He swept his Maglite across rows and rows of tilted shelves and cluttered table benches.

"Woo-hoo! Look at this cool equipment and all these ancient artifacts. It's like opening King Tut's tomb," Emily said. With her Maglite, she poked around the dark chamber. "This is better than any archaelogical dig I've ever been to."

"More like a horror movie," AJ said, motioning to Vlad. "Come on in."

Vlad shook his head. "Nay! Bad memories. Bad memories."

AJ pushed the iron door wide open and propped an old wooden stool in front of it. He wasn't about to have anyone slam the door shut on them a second time.

Vlad let out a low growl. "I'll man the lookout fer ye, mateys."

"Thanks," AJ said, slipping over to Emily.

Emily wrote her name in the layers of dust on an oblong, wooden table draped in centuries of cobwebs. "Get a load of this microscope. Archaic." She wiped its eyepiece with the cuff of her sweatshirt and peered through it. Her head popped up. "Check out these beakers! And test tubes…." Age-old, yellow bottles and jars holding floating specimens of weird-looking amphibious creatures lined the shelves, casting eerie shadows on the wall. "Cool," Emily said. "Ideas for our science project."

A faded skull and crossbones was inked on some of the bottles. "Don't touch the chemicals," AJ said. "They might be poisonous."

Emily reached across one of the benches and picked up one of the specimen jars. Using one finger, she rubbed off the layers of dirt and studied the label. The jar slipped from her grasp. She shrieked as shattering glass echoed throughout the cave-like room. "What is it? Is it alive?"

AJ looked closer. An egg-yolk-sized glob jiggled on the floor like gelatin. "Looks like an eyeball."

Vlad poked his head into the lab. "Thar be the eye of Captain One-Eyed Blackjack. A fierce pirate was he. A' course that depended on which ship ye be sailing on."

"How did it end up in Bela's lab?"

Vlad stood and crossed his small arms. He pressed his shoulder against the brick door frame. "After the Captain lost his life in a battle off shore, his eye was plucked out by the blade of a hook-hand. One night, his bloody eyeball became high gambling stakes in a game of checkers at the Shipwreck Inn." Vlad squawked, "King me! King me!"

Emily interrupted, "So, Bela won?"

Vlad scratched his back against the door frame. "Nay! The blacksmith be the lucky winner, but then he got greedy and lost the Captain's eye in a game of cards to Bela."

"Your uncle collected some weird stuff," said Emily. She stopped in front of an even larger jar and shined the light through its grimy glass.

"Watch out!" AJ teased. "Might be the Captain's other eye."

"If it is, it'd be the one made of glass," said Vlad.

"There's no liquid in this one," Emily said. "Feathers. Only feathers."

"Avast, lubbers!" Vlad dropped to all fours. "Those be mine!"

AJ stepped to the door. "Come and get 'em." He tempted Vlad to cross over the threshold and enter the lab.

Vlad clawed forward, then quickly retreated. He wiped a tear with the back of his tiny hand. "Last time I was in this lab," he choked up, "I went in as a beautiful, plumed parrot, and when I awoke I found meself trapped in this blasted rodent's vessel." Vlad squeezed his eyes tight. His body trembled.

AJ squatted down to Vlad's level. "Are you okay?"

Vlad flapped his arms as though preparing to fly. He opened his eyes and lowered his head into his paws. "How I envy the seagulls outside these prison walls."

AJ took the jar of feathers from Emily, opened its lid and placed the jar on its side. He rolled it slowly toward the rat.

Vlad's nose twitched. His wiry whiskers moved up and down. "Me feathers. Me lovely feathers." He reached inside, plucked out several colorful plumes, then sniffled and rubbed them against his bristly face.

AJ was close enough to Vlad to see lumpy surgical scars visible on his tiny head. "You *were* once a parrot!"

"Aye. I can almost feel the salty sea air ruffling me wings," Vlad reminisced.

He gently patted Vlad's head. "Say, can I ask you something? How old are you? I mean, shouldn't you be...."

"Dead?" Vlad finished AJ's thought. "Aye, me parrot self died the summer of 1698, but me brain lives on. Bela messed up when he transplanted me parrot brain into this blasted rat's head. He muddled up the aging process so I be cursed to live as a rat forever."

AJ didn't know what to say.

Vlad's quiet sniffles turned to sobs. "I'd be better off marooned on a deserted island."

A lump swelled in AJ's throat. He felt partly responsible for Vlad's unfortunate curse. After all, it had been a Zantony who had caused it.

"Omigosh!" Emily squealed. "Omigosh! Bingo!"

AJ leaned into the lab. "What?"

"I found it!"

"The treasure?"

"No. Bela's scientific notebook. And look. It's full of his old experiments." She waved the leather volume above her head as though she had just been awarded the *Young Einstein* trophy at the science fair.

"In yer hands, ye hold the answer. Now, it's up to ye to reverse the evil curse." Vlad stroked his blue and yellow feathers.

Emily joined AJ and Vlad at the lab entrance. AJ quickly filled her in on the rat's tragic tale.

Vlad glanced up at AJ and Emily and cleared his throat. "Now, I don't mean to sound ungrateful, mateys, but if ye don't mind, I'd like to be alone with me feathers."

Chapter 19

"Let's give Vlad some time alone with his feathers," AJ said.

"Things just keep getting weirder and weirder around here." Emily hugged Bela's lab book.

"Yeah," AJ agreed. "We need to figure out that riddle. Let's go back upstairs where there's better light and the air isn't so stuffy."

"And no tomb robbers to worry about," Emily said.

With his feathers clamped between his teeth, Vlad disappeared through the roots and into the passageway.

"Better lock up the lab." Emily dragged the stool aside and closed the door behind them. "Don't want anyone to steal this stuff." She pocketed the key.

"Got the journal?" AJ asked.

"Yep. And the lab notebook, too. Guarding them with my life."

AJ separated the hanging roots and they ducked back into the main tunnel.

"I can't believe we really found the lab," Emily said. "Do you realize what this means?"

The hairs on the back of AJ's neck prickled. He had a bad feeling. "Come on, let's hurry."

Emily picked up the pace. "I can't wait to read Bela's lab book. Who knows what's in it? Probably the brain transplant…how he did it and all. Vlad is the greatest science experiment in history!"

Midway through the tunnel, AJ spotted the opening in the brick wall leading back to the basement. Emily kept jabbering, but he couldn't wait to escape the tunnel.

Arrggh!

AJ gasped and swung his Maglite toward the sound. It seemed to be coming from an alcove to his right. "Run!" he screamed.

Out of the shadows, a ragged figure with a dead stare, a zombie, lunged toward them. The peg-leg skeleton rattled right behind.

"Run!" he screamed louder.

"Give me back me key, wench!" A scratchy voice erupted from the skeleton's bony jaws. The skeleton stumbled forward, waving a cutlass. It was a short, curved sword, just like the one in the book *Pirate Treasures of Craggy Cove.*

111

"Arrggh," the zombie moaned, stretching ragged arms towards AJ.

Emily tore off up the tunnel. AJ sprinted after her. Behind him, AJ felt the chill of death breathing down his neck.

At the brick opening, Emily tossed Bela's books through the hole and scrambled into the basement. "Hurry! Hurry, AJ!" she yelled from the other side.

AJ flung his Maglite behind him toward the sound of clinking bones.

Clunk!

"Arrrr! Don't let that crusty barnacle escape," the skeleton's wicked voice called, as his slicing sword struck brick, sending sparks flying.

AJ dropped to all fours and scrambled through the hole. Something grabbed his ankle and jerked him backwards. He spread his elbows and braced himself against being sucked into the hands of the monsters.

Emily screamed and yanked him forward. The grip on his ankle tugged harder.

For a split second, AJ felt like he was in a tug-of-war…a tug-of-death.

Pop!

A piercing howl echoed inside the tunnel. *"A-u-g-h-h-!"*

AJ flew into the basement. Emily shrieked and pointed.

AJ screamed, shuffling backwards. A dead, gray hand clung to his ankle. The zombie's arm had detached at the elbow and its decaying fingers were locked onto his leg.

"A-u-g-h-h-h!" The zombie howled again.

Chapter 20

AJ kicked, but the zombie's hand gripped him like a rat trap. "Get it off! Get it off!"

One by one, knuckles cracked as Emily pried each rotting finger loose.

AJ grabbed the dead hand and with one swift backhand swing, chucked it toward the tunnel. It bounced off the bricks and began crawling away. AJ kicked it through the opening.

Screeeech. Emily dragged the tattered old couch. She grunted. "Help me cover that opening."

As they blocked the hole with the couch, there was no mistaking the skeleton's scratchy voice. "This isn't over, Zantony. Ye be good as dead. There be no escaping Ozor's curse. Arrr! Heh, heh, heh."

Howls mixed with evil laughter echoed from the other side of the bricks.

AJ and Emily exchanged glances and bolted upstairs. They slammed the grim reaper door shut and slumped against it.

"Whew…." AJ caught his breath. He could still feel tightness around his ankle, but nothing was there.

"This is unreal," Emily said. "That thing lost its arm but kept coming at us."

"Zombie." AJ pressed his spine harder against the basement door.

"Now we know why your Uncle Bela sealed the tunnel."

"And we know who locked us in the crypt. Just like the coffin riddle said… *Monsters on the loose*…." AJ grabbed a kitchen chair and jammed it under the grim reaper doorknob. "We can't let them get up here." His heart raced. "Oh, no! Where's Aunt Z?"

He darted from the kitchen into the ballroom. "Aunt Z! Aunt Z!" he called, frantically searching each room, hoping she was safe.

He scrambled out to the front porch. It was dusk and there was no sign of the pink hearse. He spun around. *Bonk!* He crashed into Emily as she came out the door. "Aunt Z's gone," AJ said. "Probably running errands."

Emily glanced back inside. "Now what do we do?"

"E-e-e-e-e, E-e-e-e-e…." A high-pitched screech pierced the air.

Dark wings swooped into the porch, nicking AJ's head, before it flew out between the pillars at the opposite end.

AJ gasped. "What was that?"

"A bat!" Emily grabbed his arm, yanked him back into the house, and slammed the door. "A really big bat!"

"Could it be Count Ozor?"

"Might be," Emily said. "Just in case, we'd better stay inside."

AJ bolted toward the kitchen.

"Where are you going?" Emily shouted, right at his heels.

"To check the basement door." AJ wedged the back of the chair tighter under the glass doorknob. "That should hold them."

"Let's hope," Emily said.

In the ballroom, they flopped onto the couch, where AJ could keep an eye on the kitchen and the grim reaper door.

"We have to figure out what's going on," he said.

Emily pulled out the journal and the lab book. "In science, when you're stuck, you always go back to the beginning. Let's start with the riddle you found in the coffin."

"Right." AJ pulled the parchment out of the journal. Placing it flat on the couch between them, he read:

> *"Monsters on the loose*
> *End of a bloodline*
> *Lest a male descendent*
> *Vanquishes them*
> *Upon hallowed ground*
> *In blue moon time*
> *From a triangle of Zantonys*
> *Two times three feet deep*

A shining knight must slay
The avenging dead
By stroke of midnight
Lest more beasts rise
Thus Craggy Cove's demise."

"Here, let me see that," Emily said, reaching for it.

They swapped the riddle back and forth. While Emily studied it, AJ watched the basement door. Then he opened the lab book. "Maybe there's something in here that will help us figure out that riddle." Thumbing through the lab book's brittle pages, he came to a page that was torn. The bottom corner had been ripped away. AJ read:

"If in time the evil is freed
A dire warning you must heed
If they meet 'neath midnight moon
Zantony line is forever doomed
Incantation, the final key
Into ashes make them be
To break this vile curse of hate…."

But the words stopped at the tear.

"Bingo! It's a chant to undo the curse," Emily exclaimed. "Read the rest."

"I can't."

"Why not?"

"It's torn." AJ snapped the book shut. "What good is a chant if part of it is missing?"

The last rays of the day filtered through the round-topped stained-glass windows. AJ's gaze skipped from the three golden keys on the center pane to the church on the left pane. Then, *pow!* It hit him. The third stained-glass window didn't show a rocky hillside at all. What he'd thought were rocks and boulders were actually tombstones under a full moon.

"Read the riddle again," he said. When she finished reading, he pointed to the windows. "I think our clues are right up there." He pumped his arm. "Yessssss! Isn't that the graveyard next door?"

"You're right," Emily said.

AJ jumped up. "The riddle says we need a triangle of Zantonys!" He grabbed his skateboard. "Come on, Emily. I've got an idea, but we need to go back to the cemetery."

"What about that bat?"

"We have to risk it." AJ picked up his skateboard. "I'm taking this along. It might come in handy. Wait." He paused. "I'll be right back." He ran upstairs to his room and grabbed his bottle of Monster Spray.

Outside on the driveway, AJ shoved off on his board. Maybe riding it would help his jitters. He popped a couple *ollies* as he skimmed towards the graveyard.

Emily hustled alongside, clicking her penlight on and off. "What are you doing?"

"I've been working on a new move. I call it *Walking the Plank*. Watch this." Halfway through his routine, his nerves got the best of him and his wheels caught a rock. He bailed. "Buzzard butts!"

"If you'd been walking a real plank, you'd be shark bait," Emily said, as AJ glided under the archway and into the cemetery.

"Rather be eaten by a shark than a zombie," AJ said as he rolled forward on a packed-dirt path between the headstones. He practiced *Walking the Plank* again before reaching the mausoleum. He wiped out on the kickflip. "I'm going to land this…even if it kills me."

Emily stopped. "Omigosh! The Zantony mausoleum looks exactly like the one in the stained-glass window!"

"Just like I thought." He tucked his skateboard under his arm.

"*Two times three feet deep*," Emily recited. "Bingo! A six-foot grave. We're looking for graves."

AJ glanced around the cemetery. "A triangle of Zantony graves. We need to find three Zantony headstones that make the shape of a triangle."

They darted in and out of the headstones looking for the Zantony name.

"Here's one. Borghe Zantony," Emily said, excitedly.

"Serai Zantony!" shouted AJ, pointing at another one. He scrambled from tombstone to tombstone, crunching on dead leaves. "I don't see any more. Do you?"

"It's getting too dark to read the inscriptions."

Shadows draped across the headstones. The wind kicked up and whistled through barren branches. Ocean surf pounded beyond the cliffs. Seagulls circled above them, screeching like banshees.

Crunch. Crunch.

AJ's heart stopped. *The zombie.*

Bright headlights swept across the graveyard and tires crunched up Aunt Z's driveway. *A car.* He sighed, relieved.

"My mom's here," Emily said. "I gotta go."

The lights from the car lit up the mausoleum.

"Look!" AJ pointed. There it was, engraved in huge, bold letters: 'ZANTONY.' "The mausoleum is the third point of the triangle. That only leaves one more part to the riddle—the blue moon."

Emily gulped. "Which is tomorrow night."

Chapter 21

On Halloween, moments before the Monster Ball, Aunt Zsofia pushed AJ into her costume shop. "Hurry up and change into your costume. My guests are arriving." Aunt Zsofia flitted out the door. "It's showtime!"

AJ stared at the lame scarecrow outfit that Aunt Z had laid out on the bench next to the dressing room. He tugged the orange plaid pants over his jeans. Too tight. Too short. Too ugly. This isn't going to work, he thought. He stepped in front of the mirror. *Ridiculous.* He bent over and pulled the pant legs downward. *R-i-p-p-p.* The entire butt seam split as the door burst open.

A medieval executioner and a giant whoopee cushion charged into the costume shop.

"You're not gonna wear that, are you?" the whoopee cushion asked, making loud farting noises. AJ recognized the voice of his friend Freddy.

The executioner laughed, peeling off his hood. It was Michael.

"You look like a geek," Freddy said.

"No kidding," AJ said, flashing his ripped rear end.

"Why don't you wear this?" Freddy grabbed a pink tutu from the rack and waved it in AJ's face.

"Ha-ha. Very funny." AJ glanced at the rest of the costumes hanging in the shop. Not much left to choose from. A leprechaun suit. A French maid outfit. A pioneer dress and bonnet.

"Hey, how about that suit of armor?" Michael suggested.

"It's just a display," AJ said.

"I bet it fits," Freddy said. "Come on, we'll help you put it on."

Michael handed him the chain mail tunic and pants. AJ ripped off the scarecrow bottoms. Michael and Freddy lowered the vest of armor over his head and tightened its leather straps under his arms.

Clank. Clank. Clank. Freddy dragged the metal pants over to the bench. "You're going to have to climb up and step in."

Suddenly, Little Bo Peep popped her head into the room. "AJ, Aunt Z says not to dawdle." Behind her, the song *The Purple People Eater* blasted above the chatter of the crowd.

"Go find your sheep," AJ said.

"Who's that?" Freddy asked after Bo Peep left in a huff.

"Jaz, my annoying cousin."

"She's kinda cute," Michael said.

"You need glasses," AJ said, climbing onto the bench and staring into the hollow of the armor pants.

"You're gonna get a wedgie in these, for sure." Freddy smirked.

AJ shrugged.

"Yeah, and we'll need a can opener to get you out," Michael added.

AJ jumped off the bench. "No way. Forget the tin-can bottoms. I'll just wear the tunic, vest and helmet." He pulled off the chain mail pants, leaving his jeans on.

Freddy handed AJ the helmet. "Come on, let's go. I'm starved."

"Go on. I'll be there in a second."

Michael opened the door. "I want another candy eye-ball."

Freddy yelled back at AJ, imitating Aunt Zsofia's high-pitched voice, "Remember. No dawdling." And they were out the door.

AJ slipped the helmet onto his head and lowered the face guard. Through the eye slits, he caught a glimpse of himself in the shop mirror. The light from the chandelier glinted off his armor. He lifted the face guard and stared at his reflection.

"Oh, man. This can't be real!" Chills slithered down his spine. He reached into his pocket and pulled out the riddle from the coffin. "*...a shining knight must slay the aveng-*

ing dead by stroke of midnight...." He looked back at the mirror and gasped. "Oh, dragon crap! I *am* the knight." The riddle dropped from his hands just as the Craggy Cove bell tower tolled eight o'clock.

AJ felt as cold as ice. Four hours until midnight.

Chapter 22

AJ peeked into the ballroom. Ghosts and monsters munched and mingled. His cousin Jaz watched as Michael juggled candy eyeballs and caught them in his mouth. Freddy was first in line for a photo in the coffin.

Where's Emily? AJ thought. Where were Count Ozor, Stumpy the skeleton, and Musky the zombie? He hoped they wouldn't show up to fulfill Ozor's curse. But his sixth sense screamed at him. They'll be here. They'll be here tonight. The monsters *are* coming.

The DJ played one Halloween song after another. A man in a *Phantom of the Opera* mask took tickets at the door. Three witches stirred cauldrons by one of the fireplaces, reciting Shakespeare's *Macbeth*:

"Double, double, toil and trouble
Fire burn and cauldron bubble
Fillet of a fenny snake
In the cauldron boil and bake."

Between the shrunken heads hanging from the sconces was a sign: *Shrunken Heads Don't Kiss and Tell.*

The vampire from the monster troupe nibbled at Aunt Zsofia's neck. "You're just my type." He bared his fangs. Aunt Z giggled.

Near the refreshments, a woman in white shrieked. In the center of the table, on a silver platter, a bald man's head with bulging eyes and blackened teeth laughed.

AJ cut through the long line of guests who were waiting to be photographed inside the coffin. It seemed that every other person in line was dressed as a skeleton, a zombie, or a vampire. What a perfect place for the real monster pirates to blend in, he thought. His gut told him they'd be here biding their time until midnight when the count's curse would begin. How could he ever spot the real monsters among all these costumes? And what would he do when he found them? This wasn't going to be easy.

AJ clanked into the kitchen. He glanced at the grim reaper door. The chair was still tucked under the doorknob. "Anyone have some garlic?" he asked.

The caterers laughed. "Sure is a courageous knight who has to have his garlic ready for the vampires tonight," a plump server said.

125

If they only knew.

The server handed AJ a string of garlic and whispered in his ear, "I have one, too. Just in case."

"Thank you." AJ forced a smile. After tying the garlic around his neck, he tucked it inside his armor vest. Then he slipped up the old servant staircase that led to the hall upstairs. He entered Aunt Zsofia's bathroom where he borrowed a compact mirror, a silver cross, and a small empty spray bottle. He stuffed the objects into his pocket and slipped into his bedroom where he filled the bottle with Monster Spray. Now he was prepared. Would they work? Only time would tell.

I need to talk to Vlad, AJ thought. "Vlad, are you here?" he called. He peeked under the armoire. "Vlad, I need to talk to you." No answer. "I know you're here. Please come out. I need your help."

"Walk the plank, ye scallywag." The rat appeared behind AJ.

"Vlad, I can't do this alone. I need to know something. Is Ozor here? How will I recognize him?"

"There be no turning back now, Zantony. All's been set in motion. Ozor thirsts for bloody revenge and it will unfold at midnight."

"Help me stop them," AJ begged.

"Sorry, mate, ye be on yer own," Vlad said, scuttling under the armoire.

Vlad's words triggered an icy shiver inside AJ's armor. He tapped his helmet against the wall. "Vlad. Vlad."

No answer.

He's gone.

AJ trembled so hard the chain mail tunic clinked against his armor vest. He felt the weight of the curse as he slugged down the stairs and into the ballroom, where throngs of costumed guests danced to *Blue Moon.*

Aunt Zsofia whirled in the middle of the crowd. She was dressed as a fairy godmother. Her hair sparkled a lime green. Her shoes glittered like gold. Laughing, she waved her wand, scattering fairy dust on everyone near her.

It's Aunt Zsofia's big night. He didn't want to ruin it for her. But if Ozor has his way, AJ thought, this would be Aunt Zsofia's last Ball. It could all be destroyed at midnight. He glanced across the crowd, spotting Michael, Freddy, Jaz, his friends, teachers, and neighbors. Everyone he cared about in Craggy Cove was there and they had no idea of the danger they were in. AJ choked. *I can't let that happen!*

He had to stop Ozor and his henchmen, and the first step was to find them. He needed Emily's help, but where was she?

Three green Frankenstein monsters, with tall foreheads and neck pegs, barged through the front door and headed straight for the cookie trays. They grabbed handfuls of green witches' fingers and coconut spider nests.

AJ watched the Frankensteins. *Who are they?* His gut clenched.

A movement in the chandelier caught AJ's attention. From among the mummified bats and cobwebs hanging above the crowd, one bat turned its head toward AJ, hissed and bared its razor sharp fangs.

It's Count Ozor! Dang! Stumpy and Musky must be here, too. He had to keep them from gathering in the grave-yard at midnight.

The grandfather clock struck nine o'clock. *Three hours to go.*

AJ pushed through the crowds in the front and back yards, searching for Stumpy and Musky. He crossed the terraces and patio. Ghost lanterns and tiki torches lit the paths. Out front, Jack-o-lanterns lined the walkways and fences. He stared at the darkened cemetery. It was empty and quiet.

A mad scientist with white, scared-straight hair zigzagged up the driveway in AJ's direction. Who was it?

"Is that you, AJ?" the scientist asked. "You're an awesome knight. That armor suits you."

AJ recognized Emily's voice. "I should have known it was you. Great hair!"

Emily wore goggles, a white lab coat and black rubber fishing boots. She carried a lab notebook and a test tube of green goop foaming with dry ice. "I'm ready to mix up any concoction you want." She jiggled the test tube under his nose. The swirling vapors tickled his nostrils.

"Later." He grabbed her elbow. "Hurry. Follow me." In-side the ballroom, he pointed at the chandelier. "Ozor is swing-ing above us."

Emily pushed her goggles up.

Ozor snarled and spat at her.

She jolted back, dropping her test tube, green goop splattering at her feet. "Yikes!"

"Don't worry about it," AJ said. "The whole place will be a shipwreck before tonight's over."

She pulled up her collar and glanced around. "Have you seen the zombie and skeleton?"

"I haven't seen them yet, but they're here. I can feel it."

"Let's not waste any time. I'll help you search," Emily said. "You keep watch in here. I'll check out back."

A short time later, Emily rushed towards AJ. Nearly out of breath, she mumbled, "I found that stinking zombie pirate, Musky. He's in the gazebo. Come on."

"Maybe we can trap him and keep him away from Ozor," AJ said.

"Hurry, before we lose him," said Emily.

Out back, a mob stomped and mashed to the theme from *Ghostbusters*. AJ and Emily jostled through the crowd.

"There he is." Emily pointed to a zombie-like creature slumped over inside the gazebo. "Now what?"

AJ said, "Maybe we can trick him into the garden shed."

"How?"

"I have some garlic. Let's see if it works." AJ pulled out his string of garlic from his vest and dangled it in front of the creature's face. The zombie moaned.

Slowly the zombie rose. Oily gray hair sprang from the sides of its head. Sunken blood-shot eyes gaped at AJ. Its stiff arms batted at the clumps of garlic. It grunted like a wild boar.

AJ swung the string of garlic and pulled out Aunt Zsofia's silver cross.

The zombie's mouth hung open. Dirty brown teeth dripped saliva. The zombie shuffled forward, lumbering from side to side as it jerked towards AJ.

AJ held the garlic and cross between him and the zombie. *How could I have forgotten to bring matches or a lighter? Zombies hate fire.*

The zombie edged forward, closer and closer. Its outstretched hands opened and closed in rhythm to AJ's beating heart.

His brain screamed 'Run,' but his legs wobbled like Gummy Worms. "I'm dead meat." He squeezed his eyes shut as the zombie lunged forward and grabbed him.

Chapter 23

"Gotcha!" the zombie shrieked.

AJ stumbled backwards.

The zombie chuckled and lumbered away, his ragged laughter echoing across the yard.

"Omigosh!" Emily let out a breath. "He's just one of the monsters your aunt hired for the party."

"Whew," AJ said. "I could've sworn that was Musky."

"I thought he was real," Emily said. "I should've known it wasn't Musky. This guy has two hands. Let's keep looking."

If I freak at a fake zombie, AJ thought, how am I going to face one who's already tried to rip my leg off?

He and Emily returned to the ballroom. Immediately he glanced up at the chandelier and met the bat's beady stare. Its red eyes bore into him like a hot laser. AJ's insides felt like mushy spaghetti. He jerked his eyes away. Across the room, the old grandfather clock chimed ten o'clock. *Two hours to go.*

A growing crowd waited to step inside the coffin to have their souvenir photos taken. A rowdy conga line weaved through the ballroom and snaked out the front door.

"I thought your aunt said she only had one skeleton," Emily said, as they zigzagged behind the DJ's sound equipment.

In the corner of the graveyard scene, a sinister-looking skeleton hung its arm over Mrs. Bones' clavicle.

"Uh-oh!" AJ exchanged worried glances with Emily.

"Do you think it's Stumpy?" she asked.

"Does it have a peg leg?"

"We need a closer look," Emily said.

They threaded their way through the dancers, toward the skeletons. A Cinderella in a hoop skirt blocked AJ's view. He waited until she twirled out of the way. His stomach curdled. There it was, the peg leg.

"Stumpy!" AJ tensed.

Stumpy tilted his skull in AJ's direction, slowly flashing a bony grin. His gold tooth glinted in the strobe light as he shot AJ an icy glare.

Emily gulped. "That's him."

Fear knotted in AJ's chest. "Somehow we have to keep him from leaving."

"As long as he's flirting with Mrs. Bones," Emily whispered, "he won't go anywhere."

"Hopefully," AJ added. His eyes darted from Stumpy to Ozor. "The zombie's gotta be here, too."

"It won't be easy finding him." Emily trembled. "This place has turned into zombie central."

"We better split up," AJ said.

"Okay, but meet me on the front porch in ten minutes."

"Right. Be careful."

AJ pushed through the crowded ballroom, bumping into a whacky girl in a hospital gown with a fake butt sticking out the open back. He passed a crocodile with a rubber hand hanging from its mouth and an old man with gray hair and bushy eyebrows peeking out of a cardboard outhouse.

His cousin, Little Bo Peep, followed Michael, the executioner, like a lost sheep. Michael stopped at the table where the boo-berry punch was served and handed Bo Peep a cup.

At the front door AJ glanced back inside, making one last check on Stumpy and Ozor. They hadn't budged, but their eyes followed him.

On the porch, a shrivel-faced zombie slouched in Aunt Z's spider-web hammock. With a smelly belch, the zombie sprang toward AJ. His rubber mask and Reeboks were a dead giveaway.

"Nice try, dead dude." AJ leaned over the porch rail and scoped out the cemetery. Where was the real Musky?

In the distance, dogs howled. A dark shadow floated over Aunt Z's wall and into the graveyard. AJ jumped the porch railing. He leaned over the stone wall and peered into the blackness of *Eternal Repose*.

The shadow turned out to be just an empty trash bag blowing between the tombstones. Spooked by a plastic bag, AJ thought.

Thwonk! Thwonk! On Aunt Zsofia's rooftop, the gargoyles rocked wickedly. Their shapes were silhouetted against the shifting clouds. A full moon hovered just above their wingtips. Their stony stares crippled him.

AJ staggered back inside the house. His mind blurred. Music thrummed. Around him ghosts moaned, witches cackled, children giggled. Giddy revelers jostled and bumped him. And more costumed zombies lumbered past him than he could shake a string of garlic at.

Where's Emily? She hadn't met him on the porch. Had she found Musky? Or—worse—had Musky found her?

He scouted the room, but there was no sign of her. His heart pounded in his ears.

Aunt Zsofia grabbed his arm. "There you are. No wonder I couldn't find you. I've been looking all over for a scarecrow. You look dashing." Aunt Z pulled back. Her eyes widened. "Is that my suit of armor?"

He nodded, trying to think of a way to escape.

"Just don't dent it," she said, guiding him to the center of the dance floor. "Now come on, I have to have at least one monster mash with my nephew."

Not now, Aunt Z.

She kicked up her heels, stomped, pounded, and whooped, while he tried to break away. But she yanked him back and danced some more.

When the song ended, Aunt Zsofia whirled away. AJ spotted Emily waving her arms frantically. He hurried over.

"Is that Musky?" she asked.

Under the stained-glass windows stood a lop-sided zombie, its mouth locked in a vicious snarl, and its head drooping in the same direction as its half-rotted face. Slowly, he raised his severed arm.

The zombie from the tunnel! AJ caught a whiff of the graveyard reek. There was no doubt. It was the same monster that had attacked him.

"That's all three." AJ shivered. "But how do we keep them out of the graveyard?"

"I don't think it's going to be easy." Emily clicked her penlight on and off.

Outside, the church bells tolled. Eleven o'clock. *One hour to go.*

Sweat trickled down his back, and his chain mail felt as tight as a strait jacket. Time was ticking away. Maybe he could lock either the zombie or the skeleton in the downstairs bathroom and guard the door until midnight.

"Quick! Help me trick Musky into the bathroom," he said to Emily. "With his reek, that'll keep people away."

"How can we lure him in there without him attacking you again?" she asked.

Before he could answer, the DJ pulled him aside. "You've been selected to judge the costume contest. The ten finalists are lined up on the back terrace."

"No. Not now."

135

The DJ slapped an orange ribbon on AJ's armored vest. Black letters spelled out 'JUDGE.' "Come on. Your aunt says don't dawdle."

He groaned.

"Just hurry and get it over with," Emily blurted.

On his way out back, he glanced over his shoulder at Ozor and the other dead pirates. All three monsters hissed at him. "Please," he begged Emily. "Don't let them out of your sight."

The DJ dragged AJ to a platform where two other judges stood. One was a robust King Henry the Eighth and the other was a giant Coca-Cola bottle.

King Henry the Eighth said, "In my mind, the winner is Anne Boleyn."

The Coca-Cola bottle bubbled. "Nah, she's still got her head on. Personally, I like the Queen of Hearts. I'll have to ask her where she got her shoes. Ha, even the Volcano is a blast. No one erupts like that and dances at the same time."

The king chuckled and swung his royal robe. "Well, Sir Knight, what do you think?"

"Whatever," AJ said.

The king patted AJ's shoulder, rattling his armor. "Wake up, dodo brain. Who do you want to award First Prize to?"

AJ panned the ten finalists. "The spider," he muttered.

The king and the bottle looked at the giant hairy spider. "Which legs are human and which are fake?" the king asked.

"Awesome costume," the bottle agreed. "Okay, I'll vote for the spider."

"The spider wins," the king said. "I'll tell the DJ to announce it." King Henry the Eighth marched towards the back door. The Coca-Cola bottle waddled behind.

A gust of wind as cold as an icicle swept over the backyard, swinging the paper lanterns and scattering paper plates across the lawn.

An evil chill pierced AJ's armor. He looked up. The moon was cloaked in a somber dark cloud. Something was watching him. He sensed it. *Was it the house?* He searched its darkened upstairs windows. Nothing.

Above him, the rooftop gargoyles spread their enormous wings and glowered at him. Slowly they shifted to face the graveyard. Trembling, AJ darted back inside.

Tick-tock. Tick-tock. The grandfather clock said eleven-ten. *Fifty minutes till midnight.*

"What took so long?" Emily asked.

AJ eyed Ozor, who was still hanging upside-down from the chandelier. The bat stretched its wings. "Oh, no. It's happening," AJ said in a strong whisper. "He's getting ready to fly! We gotta stop them."

"I'll watch Ozor, while you...," she started.

Out of nowhere, three Frankenstein monsters cut them off and blocked them from leaving the ballroom. The tallest one slammed AJ's face guard down. "Look at the wimpy knight and geeky scientist."

"No, she's a nutty professor," said another.

"It's Calvin, Dirk, and Runt!" Emily exclaimed. "What are you goon-heads doing here?"

"We're having a little fun." It was Dirk's voice.

AJ pushed his face guard up. The tall one, Calvin, slammed it down again.

"Hey, stop it," AJ said.

"Whatsamatta, Prince Charmin'? Can't ya keep your helmet on straight?" Calvin twisted the helmet on AJ's head so it now faced backwards.

"Look, da poor knight can't see," Dirk said.

"Stop it! I have something I have to do." AJ tugged at his helmet.

"What you gotta do? Slay a dragon?" Runt chided.

"None of your business," Emily said. "Just leave us alone! We have to go."

"Goo-goo, gaa-gaa," Calvin babbled. "Crawl away, Baby-kins, before you wet your pants and leave a puddle."

"You gonna let 'em go?" Runt asked.

"Yeah. Let's go pig out. We can have fun with 'em later." Calvin sneered. "See you later, boney Zantony."

As soon as the bullies were gone, AJ tugged at his helmet. "Quick. We're running out of time. Help me get this off."

Emily lifted AJ's helmet off.

He checked the clock. *Forty-five minutes until midnight.* "Emily. The monsters? Where are they?"

The skeleton and zombie were nowhere in sight. Above them, the chandelier swayed. Ozor was gone.

Chapter 24

Emily grabbed AJ's arm. "Now what?"

He locked eyes with her. "The graveyard! We've got to get to the graveyard. I *have* to stop them, somehow." He stormed through the conga line and out the front door, calling to Emily. "C'mon. We're losing time."

On the porch, he reached below the spider-web hammock where he'd left his skateboard. He spun around and nearly knocked Emily down the steps.

A purple-lipped clown with a glowing cigarette dangling from his painted mouth heckled, "Hey, kids! Where's the fire?" He reached into his polka-dot coat pocket and tossed a fistful of confetti into the air as AJ and Emily hurried past.

AJ spat flakes of paper that caught on his lip.

"I hate clowns!" Emily said. "I always wonder what they're hiding under their makeup."

Beyond the driveway, AJ plunked his skateboard down, tucked his helmet under his armpit like a football, then hopped onto his board. With one foot he shoved off, propelling himself toward the moonlit graveyard.

His armor clink-clanked as he whooshed along the sidewalk. A hairpin turn later, he rolled through the *Eternal Repose* gates, where gnarled oaks hunched over like decrepit old men, their branches clawing at him as he whizzed by.

Emily's lab coat flapped in the breeze as she kept up.

In front of the mausoleum, three looming figures blocked AJ's path.

"Watch out! The monsters!" Emily shrieked.

AJ skidded to a bumpy stop. His armored helmet sailed through the air and crashed into a headstone. His skateboard slammed up against the stone mausoleum. He tumbled to the ground and tasted dirt.

Emily screamed. "Let go of me, you maggot-breath moron!"

AJ looked up to see Emily sink her teeth into Frankenstein's bulging arm.

"Ouch!" Calvin shouted. "You dogface freak-a-zoid! Eat worms and die!" He threw Emily down. Her goggles slipped off her head and she landed on her back near AJ's feet.

"Are you all right?" AJ asked. He heard her whimper and catch her breath as Calvin and his cronies celebrated with high-fives. Emily scooched backwards, joining AJ at the mausoleum. They sat on the ground with their backs pressed against the cold stone.

"What are we going to do now?" Emily whispered.

"I don't know. I'm thinking. I'm thinking." He gasped and pointed. "Look. Count Ozor." A bat clung to the marble wing of an angel statue guarding the grave of Borghe Jöska Zantony.

"I see him," Emily said. "But where are Stumpy and Musky?"

"Oh, no!" AJ yelped.

Calvin, Dirk, and Runt closed in on them like a pack of dogs beneath a werewolf moon.

"Hiding behind your girly-ghoul?" Calvin taunted.

AJ scrambled to his feet and faced Calvin. "We don't have time for you!"

"Buzz off!" Emily said, standing next to AJ. "We've got real monsters to deal with!"

"What do you know, the Great Zantony is going to save us all from the big, bad, scary monsters!" Calvin's legs wobbled like rubber bands.

"Did you bring your Monster Spray?" Dirk snorted and sucked in snot.

Runt knuckle-fived Dirk and said, "I know. He's going to scare them away with that hideous Halloween mask he's wearing. Oh, that's not a mask. It's his real face!"

"Good one!" Calvin said.

A cloud crossed the moon, darkening the graveyard and cloaking them in deep shadows. Below the cliffs, breaking waves roared. As the clouds cleared, moonlight washed across the tombstones.

Calvin's shadow hulked over AJ as he swaggered forward. AJ knew Calvin wasn't going to back off, but *he* wasn't backing down this time.

Calvin shoved AJ's shoulders. AJ stumbled backwards, recovered, and took a boxing stance, his fists near his jaw.

"Fight! Fight! Fight!" Dirk and Runt climbed onto tombstones and cheered.

"Back off, zombie zit!" Emily yelled.

Calvin flicked AJ's ears. "Ain't that sweet. Now your girlfriend is fighting your battles."

AJ pulled back his arm, ready to strike, but before he could make his move, Calvin's knuckles crunched against his metal vest.

"Ow!" Calvin writhed. "My fingers! They're busted!"

Dirk and Runt snickered as they leaped off the headstones.

Calvin looked at them, eyes bulging. "You two cockroaches think it's funny? Come over here! I'll squash you!"

"I wasn't laughing," Dirk said, gulping his chuckles. "I was coughing…see?" He faked a coughing fit.

"Yeah, man. Me, too." Runt hacked so hard, he looked like a cat about to huck a hair ball.

Calvin smacked Dirk and Runt on their foreheads, then turned his squinty gaze back to AJ and Emily. "So, Mr. Monster Slayer, where's your big, bad monster?"

"Partying with his freaky aunt," said Runt.

AJ pointed at the angel statue. "There's one now!"

"Where?" Swinging his shoulders, Calvin strutted over to the statue. "You wuss. That's a fruit bat. What an idiot."

The bat launched and flitted about Calvin's face. He ducked. "Get it away! Get it away!"

With bare hands, Dirk and Runt batted at the flying demon.

AJ and Emily rushed into the Zantony triangle of tombstones. Ozor disappeared into rustling treetops.

Calvin ordered his troops, "Quick! Don't let Monster Boy escape!"

Dirk grabbed AJ, and Runt caught Emily.

"Let go of me, Frankenturd!" Emily squirmed.

"What should we do with them? Bury them?" asked Runt, holding onto Emily's lab coat collar. Dirk held AJ in a back arm lock.

Calvin skulked over to the mausoleum door. "Nah, I have a better idea. Bring 'em here!" AJ and Emily kicked all the way. "You two want to play monsters? Well, there's plenty of ghosts in here to keep you company." Calvin laughed and shoved AJ and Emily into the mausoleum and began to close the door.

AJ struggled against the door's heavy weight, trying to keep it open, but the door slammed shut like a stone coffin lid, leaving them in suffocating darkness.

Chapter 25

"This is just like my nightmare!" AJ howled.

Outside, Calvin hollered, "Drag that bench over here."

"What bench?" Dirk asked.

"The cement bench, you dill weed," Calvin yelled.

AJ rammed his shoulder against the door.

"Let us out!" Emily shrieked. "This is life or death!" With double fists, she pounded on the door. "Open up!"

AJ heard a loud thump followed by a sickening scrape. The cement bench, he thought. The cronies had blocked the door with the cement bench. His stomach heaved. He tasted barf in the back of his throat.

Then he heard Calvin's muffled voice. "Nighty night, Ghosty Boy."

"Yeah, rest in peace, losers," Dirk added, banging the door from the other side. Suddenly the ruckus stopped. Emily clicked on her penlight, skipping its narrow beam from wall to wall.

"Listen. They're gone," she said, her ear pressed against the door.

AJ slammed his body armor into the door one last time. It wouldn't budge. He slumped to the floor, lowering his head into his hands. "I blew it. Now there's no one to stop Count Ozor."

"Wait! The secret passage!" Emily said. "Remember?"

"Oh, yeah," AJ said. "But, what if Stumpy and Musky are in there?"

Emily's penlight flickered. "Oh, no! Not now!"

AJ heard her tap it against the wall. The last flicker of light disappeared.

"It's dead," she said.

"And dark. It's like being blind."

"What'll we do now?"

"The grate!" AJ exclaimed. "If we can just find that grate that leads to the crypt…." He took a step and bumped into Emily.

"Ouch!" she said. "But what about the monsters?"

"We'll have to risk it." Hand over hand, AJ inched along the cold marble walls. "You'll have to feel your way," he said.

"Wait. Did you hear that?" Emily said.

"What?"

"Scratching."

He listened hard. Between clenched teeth, he sucked in stale air. Could another corpse be clawing its way out of a tomb? How many more zombies were entombed in these walls?

"Avast mateys!"

"Vlad!" Emily said, letting out a rush of breath. "You're here."

"Can you help us get out?" AJ asked. "We can't see a thing."

"Aye. But make haste. Ye be runnin' out of time. Follow me voice."

"Thanks, Vlad," AJ said. "I thought we were doomed."

"If ye be doomed, then I be doomed, too. Walk the plank, awk!" chanted Vlad. "Walk the plank!" he squawked over and over.

"Walk the plank? Vlad, can you sing something else?" Emily said. "We're terrified as it is. We don't know where the monsters are, and you make it sound like we're going to plunge to our deaths."

"Yeah, don't jinx us," AJ said. "Just lead us out of here."

From behind, Emily held onto AJ's shoulders. He held his hands out in front of him as they took baby steps through the darkness.

"At this pace, it'd be mornin' before ye finds yer way out," Vlad said.

"Sorry," said AJ, "but we don't have rat vision."

"Avast! Aye, here be the grate. Stoop, and down the hatch ye go."

AJ crouched and felt around for the waffle pattern of the iron grate.

Emily helped AJ grasp the grate and they shoved it aside. AJ rolled onto his stomach and dropped his legs over the ledge. "Here goes nothing," he said, taking a deep breath. He clung onto the ledge and lowered himself.

"Easy," Emily said.

"I can't feel the bottom." AJ's voice echoed into the darkness.

"The step be a whisker's length from yer toes," Vlad said. "Be careful when ye land. The steps be crumbling."

AJ dropped to the top step, which gave way beneath him. He pitched forward, his armor clanking all the way down.

Emily landed on top of him.

"Ooomph!" He saw stars.

"Ow, that hurt," Emily moaned.

"That's what I call stepping up the pace. Now, on yer feet, mates," Vlad ordered. "I gots me own hole to fit through, but ye must open the secret wall."

AJ struggled to stand. The smell of rotting zombie guts led them to the opening. He braced against the wall and felt for the sliding doorway back to the crypt. He pushed and it hissed open. They squeezed through.

"Awk! Musky's been here. His rotten stench lingers," Vlad said.

Emily gagged. "Get us out of here."

"Uh-oh. We're trapped," AJ said. "Don't you remember? The crypt door doesn't have a handle on the inside."

Chapter 26

"We're stuck. Again," Emily said.

"Would I lead ye to a dead end, mateys?" asked Vlad. "Pull on the sconce to the right of the door, three bricks over."

AJ found the sconce and yanked it. The door creaked open.

"Holy guacamole! This place has more secrets than the Egyptian pyramids," Emily said.

AJ heard Vlad's claws scamper up the dark tunnel. "Do you think Musky and Stumpy are hiding down here?"

"I hope not…or we're good as dead," Emily said.

"But Vlad wouldn't lead us into an ambush, would he?" AJ flattened his backside against the side walls and slid in the direction of the opening in the brick archway.

"I thought we left the light on in the basement." Emily's voice was right beside him.

"We did," he said. "The couch is blocking the hole."

At the end of the tunnel, AJ squatted and felt the couch through the opening. With his back pressed to the ground he propped both feet against the back of the couch and pushed hard. The couch shifted and a faint light filtered into the tunnel. He stood up. "Ladies first."

"You *are* a chivalrous knight." Emily crawled through the hole. Vlad followed.

AJ poked his head into the basement. "Sweet." He sighed. "We made it." He wriggled forward on his belly, his armor scraping against the bricks. Next thing he knew, his armor got stuck in the opening. AJ pushed with all his might but only wedged himself in tighter, like a cat caught in a drain pipe. "Dragon crap!"

Vlad scuttled closer until he was nose to nose with AJ. "Make haste. Remember the curse. It be nearly midnight."

"The poker. Get the poker!" AJ screamed.

Emily grabbed the fireplace poker. She smashed the mortar between the bricks and the wall crumbled around AJ. He squeezed his eyes tight and held his breath as the opening widened. He dragged himself forward, releasing the smell of crushed garlic, his armor vest screeching until at last he was free.

AJ regained his footing. "I think I smashed my string of garlic," he said. "Man, Vlad, thanks for getting us out of there. You're the best."

"Awk. I got a stake in this, too. Ozor will hunt me to the ends of the earth to find the treasure of Captain One-Eyed Blackjack. So, you see, mate, I got me own reasons for ye to stop Ozor. But, now ye be on yer own."

"Aren't you coming with us?" AJ asked.

"Nay, I'll not be venturing upstairs near the hag that wants me dead."

"Aunt Zsofia wouldn't feel that way if she knew you," Emily said.

"Make haste," Vlad repeated, hopping onto the top of the old tattered couch. He pointed at them. "Don't give up the ship. Do what ye must to destroy Ozor and his vile curse. If ye don't, it be doomsday for all of us."

AJ swallowed hard. The party thumped above them. He and Emily tore up the basement stairs.

"Godspeed, mateys!" Vlad called to them before scampering back into the tunnel.

At the top of the stairs, AJ grabbed the knob of the grim reaper door and rattled it.

"Oh, no! It won't open! The chair! The chair is still wedged under the knob!"

Chapter 27

AJ and Emily stood at the top of the basement stairs.

"Is anyone in the kitchen?" Emily asked him.

"The caterers." AJ pounded on the door. Emily did, too.

The door flew open. They stumbled into the kitchen, landing at the feet of the caterer holding the chair. "I don't know who put this here." The caterer shook her head. "Strange party."

AJ and Emily burst into the ballroom. He looked at the oversized pocket watch of a man dressed as the Mad Hatter.

"Quarter to midnight!" AJ said.

"Hurry!" Emily blurted. "We only have fifteen minutes."

"Let's go out the back way so we don't run into Calvin and his cronies again," AJ suggested.

"Smart thinking," Emily said.

They shot out the kitchen door, ran around the back of the house, and stopped at the stone wall, just short of the graveyard.

"Yikes!" cried Emily, bracing herself against the wall. "I'm feeling dizzy. What is it?"

In the graveyard, the ground rolled and heaved like an angry sea. AJ stared at the rippling earth. *What if the curse is coming true and the ground is opening up and all the dead are rising to destroy Craggy Cove?*

Chapter 28

"Why is the ground moving?" Emily asked.

AJ gulped. "It's a sea of rats!"

Wave upon wave of rats swarmed the graveyard as far as AJ could see. Under the glow of the moon, thousands of rats climbed tombs and funneled between headstones.

"Oh, no, look who's back!" Emily yelled.

AJ couldn't believe his eyes. Calvin, Dirk, and Runt sprinted through the rolling ground in the cemetery, screaming and flailing their arms and bumping into grave markers. Calvin swatted at a rat crawling up his pant leg while Runt ripped a rat from his rear. Dirk took a flying leap for the wing of an angel statue. He missed. Rats swarmed over his body until he disappeared. He popped up, screeching in terror.

AJ watched as the mass of rats gathered near the mausoleum. Standing atop the Zantony mausoleum, Vlad stretched his arms wide and chattered wildly.

AJ turned to see if Emily was watching, but she was gone. "Emily," he called. "Where are you?"

"Over here!" she yelled from the driveway. Emily sat on the hood of the pink hearse, her legs pulled beneath her.

"What are you doing?"

"Rats!" She pointed to the ground. "I can't walk through them. They'll crawl up my legs."

"Did you see Calvin barreling down the street flicking rats off his head? I bet he's the one changing his doody diapers now."

Emily hugged her knees tighter and trembled. "Where did they all come from?"

"Vlad's friends, I guess. Come on. The bells haven't tolled midnight yet. We have to get to the Zantony triangle before the monsters do."

"But…the rats!"

"Can't let them stop us! Every second counts. Come on, Emily!" he yelled. "They won't bite you."

"They might," she said.

"Nah," he said. "They're busy listening to Vlad."

She sucked in a deep breath and slowly slid off the hood of the hearse. "I can do this. I can do this," she muttered as they dashed for the graveyard.

Inside the cemetery, they stopped cold. Two tall shadowy figures lumbered towards them.

"It's them," AJ half-whispered to Emily.

Musky, the zombie, walked stiff-legged, seaweed dripping from his outstretched arms. With every shuffle, he released a deep, throaty gurgle, sending chills up AJ's spine. The gut-wrenching, puke-triggering scent of a rotting corpse smothered the graveyard. Black blood oozed from the zombie's mouth as he lurched towards the Zantony triangle.

Behind Musky, the skeleton Stumpy gimped along on his peg leg. He weaved in and around tombstones, his bones rattling. As Stumpy neared the mausoleum, something glinted in the moonlight. The skeleton brandished the cutlass he'd swung at AJ in the tunnel.

AJ scanned the skies for Ozor. Instead of the count, he saw the gargoyles perched forward, as if they were spectators with front row seats at the midnight event.

With dead stares on their ugly faces, the zombie and skeleton groaned and growled as they plodded closer to the mausoleum.

AJ clenched his fists. "I'm not letting those dead pirates destroy me or my family! If I have to die stopping them, I will!"

Something touched his shoulder. He jumped.

"Just me," Emily said. "Don't worry. I got your back."

AJ nodded, afraid of taking his eyes off of Musky and Stumpy, even for a second. "I gotta keep them off the points of the triangle."

"They've got maggots for brains," Emily said. "You can outsmart them."

Still on the roof of the mausoleum, Vlad belted out another one of his pirate ditties.

> *"Three dead pirates with ruthless goals,*
> *Yeo-heave-ho, and a bottle of rum.*
> *Who'll be alive when midnight tolls?*
> *Yeo-heave-ho, and a bottle of rum."*

The words haunted AJ. Who would be alive at midnight? Their lives *really* were at stake.

AJ paced on the cement bench in front of the mausoleum at the head of the Zantony triangle. Emily scrambled up the narrow steps to join Vlad on the roof. AJ patted his pockets, relieved to feel the outlines of the mirror, silver cross, and his Monster Spray.

Vlad poked his head over the edge of the mausoleum. "Awk, matey," he said to AJ. "Them pirates have waited 300 years to seek revenge on the Zantonys. Even the gargoyles be watching. Ye can bet old Bela is rolling over in his tomb."

AJ choked up. "I don't know if I can do this, you guys."

Moving closer, Stumpy slashed the air with his cutlass while Musky spit bloody maggots.

"Where's my skateboard? Emily, can you see my board? I need it!"

Emily ran circles on the mausoleum roof, then pointed to the side of the building. "I see it. I see it. Over here! It's crawling with rats!"

AJ hopped off the bench. His skateboard and helmet lay overturned on the grass near the headstone where he had crashed earlier. He scooped up the helmet and lowered it onto his head, then tried to pull the dented face-guard down. It was stuck in the open position. With his foot, he flipped his board onto its wheels.

"Go get 'em, AJ!" Emily hollered.

"Aye," Vlad squawked. "Walk the plank, mate!"

AJ searched the skies. "Do you see Count Ozor any-where?" He leapt onto his skateboard. The army of rats parted as he zipped back to the head of the triangle. "Vlad, can your rat friends keep the monsters away from the triangle?"

The dead pirates crept closer and closer, snarling with each jerky step.

"Nothing can stop the curse from unfolding. The pirates be after Zantony blood." Vlad sniffed the air. "When Bela cursed them, aye, he knew they'd return, so he wrote a pow-erful chant to stop them."

Emily yelled, "The chant, AJ! Bela's chant! Say it! Say it! Say it!"

AJ rolled his skateboard back and forth across the eye of the triangle. "We don't have the whole thing," he shouted. "It was torn, remember?"

"Maybe it'll work without the missing part. You have no choice. You gotta try."

"Awk! Walk the plank!" yelled Vlad.

Musky shook his severed arm at AJ. "Time for pirate payback. Zantonys be doomed!" His words garbled as his tongue slopped through his rotted cheek.

"Aye." Stumpy thrashed his cutlass. "Har-har-har."

The monsters clomped their separate ways toward two corners of the triangle.

Emily screamed. "Watch out! They're almost in their positions."

AJ had to keep at least one monster away from a Zantony headstone when the clock struck midnight. He worked his skateboard back and forth, then pulling his mirror out of his pocket, recited the chant.

> *"If in time the evil is freed*
> *A dire warning you must heed*
> *If they meet 'neath midnight moon*
> *Zantony line is forever doomed*
> *Incantation, the final key*
> *Into ashes make them be*
> *To break this vile curse of hate..."*

AJ hollered, "What comes next?"

"It has to rhyme with hate," Emily shouted.

"Bait, crate, date, fate. It could be anything. There are a million words that rhyme with hate."

"Fate!" Emily shouted. "Try it!"

"And unseal the horrible fate," he said. Nothing happened.

"Arrr!" With a triumphant roar, Musky stepped up to the headstone of Borghe Zantony, the first point of the triangle.

AJ rolled as close to Musky as he dared and aimed the mirror, hoping to catch the dead pirate's image. He wasn't sure what it was supposed to do, but he hoped it would work. It didn't. Musky held his spot.

Stumpy grinned and flashed his gold tooth. With one slash of his cutlass, he chopped the cherub head off the top of Serai Zantony's tombstone, the second point of the triangle. Then, with a solid swing of his peg leg, he kicked the cherub head at AJ.

AJ dodged the stone head as it flew by like a cannonball. He slowed his skateboard and pulled back.

Dragon crap! This isn't looking good.

Chapter 29

"Keep an eye out for the count!" AJ shouted to Emily. "We can't let him sneak up on us."

"I'm watching! I'm watching!"

AJ knew he was as good as dead if Count Ozor appeared at the head of the Zantony triangle. Dead on Halloween. At a party! Was there a worse time to die?

"Try the chant again," Emily yelled.

AJ searched the graveyard for signs of Ozor and recited:

> *"If in time the evil is freed*
> *A dire warning you must heed*
> *If they meet 'neath midnight moon*
> *Zantony line is forever doomed*

Incantation, the final key
Into ashes make them be
To break this vile curse of hate…"

When he came to the last line, AJ blurted out, "Keep them apart before it's too late." Again, nothing happened.

AJ rolled towards the zombie and flashed the silver cross. Musky snorted and swatted the cross out of AJ's hand. The zombie's left eye popped from its socket and dangled below his nostril like a slimy booger.

Holding his ribcage, Stumpy hooted with laughter. His jawbone clattered so fast, two molars shot out and rolled to the ground like a pair of dice.

AJ didn't take his eyes off of Stumpy or Musky as he rolled on his board back and forth between the monsters. Still no sign of the count.

The chant. The chant. What would Bela have said?

AJ repeated the chant faster:

"If in time the evil is freed
A dire warning you must heed
If they meet 'neath midnight moon
Zantony line is forever doomed
Incantation, the final key
Into ashes make them be
To break this vile curse of hate…"

"Ummm…." His voice quivered. "I don't know. I can't figure it out."

Gargoyle shadows clawed across the mausoleum in a blur of wings and tongues and talons. The full moon glowed overhead.

AJ reeled around on his board. The front end dipped, cutting into the ground. He bailed but quickly hopped back on.

Vlad bounced up and down. "Walk the plank, mate! Walk the plank!"

Walk the Plank. My new routine? How will that help me?

Emily shouted, "Hurry, do something. Your Monster Spray. Try it."

Monster Spray. Walk the Plank. Last line of the chant. This is driving me crazy.

AJ whipped out his spray bottle. *What have I got to lose?* He choked on his thought. *Just my life!*

He rolled closer to Musky, fumbling with the bottle. The zombie growled. AJ aimed and sprayed.

Musky clawed at his face as a stream of maggots washed out of his hollow cheek. His dangling eyeball glopped to the ground and landed in the path of AJ's board.

Squirt!

"Arghhhh!" Musky roared. "First me arm, then me eye. I'll rip ye apart piece by piece and feed yer innards to the monsters of the sea." His roar echoed through the graveyard.

AJ shoved hard with his foot and rolled away. His knees wobbled and his skateboard tottered under him. Gripping his spray bottle, he dragged his toe to slow himself down. Sweeping closer to the skeleton, AJ pumped the trigger and spritzed Stumpy.

Ribs rattling and jaws clacking, Stumpy convulsed with laughter.

Slish! Slash! The cutlass swiped the air in front of AJ's face.

"Your cheek!" Emily screamed. "It's bleeding!"

AJ touched his cheek. Warm blood trickled down his neck and into his armor.

"Watch out!" Emily ducked low.

A bat flew above AJ's head, then disappeared. His stomach lurched. "It's the count!"

"Oh, no!" Emily yelled.

"What do I do?"

Vlad shook his front paws. "Awk! Walk the plank, mate!"

The bells of Craggy Cove Church began to toll.

"Midnight!" AJ gasped. Suddenly, everything was clear. He was the final player in a battle between Bela Zantony and Count Ozor, a war 300 years old. Now it all depended on him.

The skeleton threw his head back and laughed louder. "Meet yer doom, Zantony."

Emily shrieked, "Look up!"

Out of the blackness, the bat dipped and swooped over the graveyard, then hovered above the mausoleum.

"Hit the deck," Vlad ordered.

As the church bells tolled twice, the vampire bat transformed into Count Ozor and landed on the cement bench blocking the mausoleum door. He stood at the head of the Zantony triangle. The count brushed himself off, straightened his cape, then glared at AJ. Menacingly, Ozor cocked an eyebrow, twirled his moustache, and grinned.

Chapter 30

Ozor's eyes flashed blood red, searing through AJ. His armor heated. His skin burned.

Vlad yelled, "Look away from the demon eyes, mate. He'll suck the courage right out of ye."

"Ha, ha!" Ozor laughed. "Is this scrawny bilge rat the best the Zantony line has to offer?"

"Arghhh! Must've scraped the bottom of the barrel to come up with this poop deck swabber," Musky chortled, as he plugged his empty eye socket with seaweed that clung to his tattered clothes.

In the eye of the triangle, AJ spun a *360* on his skateboard. *I blew it. There's no stopping them now. They've won!*

Count Ozor, Stumpy, and Musky held fast to the three points of the Zantony triangle.

The church bells tolled three times.

"Master." Stumpy raised his cutlass and click-clacked forward. "Let me swat this pesky fly and be done with him."

"Man your post, you bumbling bottle-head," Ozor commanded.

AJ's thoughts raced, but time seemed to slow down. He wheeled a *180*, built his momentum, and rolled toward Stumpy. If he knocked the skeleton down, maybe he could keep it from its position in the triangle. Stumpy thrust his cutlass. AJ jerked sideways, dodging the blade. The tail end of his board caught Stumpy's peg leg. The skeleton tottered on one leg then clattered to the ground, losing his grip on the cutlass.

Four tolls.

AJ jumped off his board and reached for the sword, but Stumpy snatched it first. AJ grabbed the severed cherub head. Planting his feet firm, he hurled the stone head at Stumpy. The head rolled like a bowling ball, striking Stumpy before the skeleton could get to his feet. *Crack*. His tail bone fell off.

"Way to go," cheered Emily. "You're on a roll!"

The church bells tolled five.

AJ hopped on his board and swished past the zombie. Musky swiped at him, but AJ launched off the board, throwing a flying sidekick. He thrust his foot into Musky's putrified chest with such force it burst through the zombie's back. AJ yanked his leg out. Black beetles gushed from Musky's gaping chest as a morbid howl ripped from his ragged throat.

Emily shouted, "Two down, one to go!"

Six tolls.

Ozor snarled and bared his fangs. His cape snapped in the wind like a pirate flag in a hurricane. Leaves trembled around his boots.

"Don't let him near yer neck," squealed Vlad. "He'll bite ye, he'll bite ye!"

AJ tucked his chin inside the neck of the armored vest and backed away.

"Scurvy brains, get what's left of yer carcasses back into place!" Ozor yelled at Musky and Stumpy. "Don't ye move until the midnight tolls be done, ye bloody swine!"

Stumpy clawed back to his point of the triangle. Musky dragged his shredding body to his spot.

The clock struck again. Seven tolls.

"No!" Emily screamed. "They're all back in place. Hurry, try the chant again."

"Egad!" cried Vlad. "Tis the end. We be doomed, mate."

Eight tolls.

"No! No! I'm not giving up!" AJ repeated the chant:

> *"If in time the evil is freed*
> *A dire warning you must heed*
> *If they meet 'neath midnight moon*
> *Zantony line is forever doomed*
> *Incantation, the final key*
> *Into ashes make them be*
> *To break this vile curse of hate...."*

Nine tolls.

Ozor laughed. His eyes flared. "And Bela thought he could undo my curse. Ha! Any last words before ye walk the plank, mate?"

That's it! The line.

Ten tolls.

"I can do this." AJ rocketed his skateboard to the eye of the triangle. He shouted at the top of his lungs:

> *"If in time the evil is freed*
> *A dire warning you must heed*
> *If they meet 'neath midnight moon*
> *Zantony line is forever doomed*
> *Incantation, the final key*
> *Into ashes make them be*
> *To break this vile curse of hate…"*

Eleven tolls.

"Walk the plank, mate!" AJ yelled above the bong of the church bells.

A blinding flash of blue light shot from the moon, striking AJ's shiny armor. The light reflected off his vest and split into three beams. Each beam crackled and sizzled. The first bored into Stumpy. The second beam lasered Musky. The third blue beam impaled Ozor. The moonbeams held the monsters in place. The earth roared, dark clouds thundered, and the wind screamed around the Zantony triangle. The rest of the graveyard glowed an eerie midnight blue.

The final toll. Twelve midnight.

Stumpy twisted and writhed. His jaws clattered. His bones shattered and he crumpled into a heap. As he turned to ash, all that remained was his gold tooth.

"Blow the man down!" Vlad hooted.

"None of us gets the treasure now!" Musky howled, collapsing to the ground.

"Shut up, you reeking sack of burning flesh!" hissed the count.

With his one hand, Musky clawed at the moonbeam striking his chest. His clothing smoked. Pockets of his flesh boiled and bubbled.

"Nooooooo!" Musky's yowl withered as a gust of wind hurled his glowing ashes toward the cliff.

Ozor sneered at AJ, then whipped his cape like enormous dragon wings.

AJ held his breath.

Emily shouted from the mausoleum, "He's going to fly away!"

Count Ozor faced the moon as dead leaves spiraled around his legs. He flipped his cape wide over his gaunt face, his fiery eyes searing into AJ. The vampire bared his fangs. The leaves whirled around him tighter and tighter. "You have won, Zantony!" The count's voice howled from deep inside the funnel of leaves. "It will not always be sooo-o-o-o...," Ozor threatened, before he disintegrated into a pile of smoldering ash.

On top of the mausoleum, Emily danced a jig.

Vlad sang:

> *"Maggoty seadogs no longer trouble,*
> *Yeo-heave-ho, and a bottle of rum.*
> *All that be left is ash and rubble,*
> *Time to uncork that bottle of rum."*

Chapter 31

Emily rushed down the steps leading off the mausoleum roof. "Woo-hoo! You did it, AJ!" she cheered.

Vlad whooped. "That be the end of that *vampirate*!" He scurried down the ivy-covered wall to the ground and marched over to Stumpy's ashes. He plucked the gold tooth out and buffed it against his fur. "Awk. I be keepin' this for a souvenir." The gold tooth gleamed in his claws.

"Whew, it's over." AJ collapsed on the cement bench with his head in his hands.

Emily placed her hand on his shoulder. "It really is over. You did it!"

Vlad hopped up on the bench, wiggling his way between them. "Well done, me hearties. Well done!"

Emily laughed. "Yep. Well done! Fried by a moonbeam. What a way to go!"

"Better them than us," AJ said.

A Halloween breeze whistled through the graveyard, catching the remaining pirates' ashes in its wake, blowing them over the tombstones and out to sea.

"Did—did you see that?" Emily asked, glancing at AJ.

AJ nodded.

Vlad snorted. "Good riddance to ye, evil scoundrels."

The wind died and the graveyard was quiet. The gargoyles on Zala Manor stood rock still. AJ looked at the moon. The blue beams had disappeared, but a rainbow ring circled the moon like a halo. "Awesome moon!" he said.

"Yeah, Monster Moon." Emily paused. "Must be atmospheric conditions."

They stared at the blue moon. AJ took a deep breath. It was like a huge anchor lifted off his shoulders. Laughter and music wafted across the graveyard.

Emily brushed leaves off her lab coat. "Ready to go back to the party?"

"I think so." AJ stood up.

Vlad flipped the gold tooth in his paw. "I be keepin' this treasure in a safe place now."

Back inside the ballroom, AJ and Emily flopped into folding chairs.

AJ looked at the crowd. "They don't have a clue."

"I wouldn't have believed it if I hadn't seen it myself," said Emily. "AJ, you could have died."

"Everybody here could have died."

"Shhh, here comes your aunt."

Aunt Zsofia fluttered over, scattering silver fairy dust. Taking two glasses of boo-berry punch from a server's tray, she handed them to Emily and AJ. She took another glass and raised it. "Here's to the blue moon and the best Monster Ball I ever threw."

"To the blue moon." AJ clinked his glass with Emily's. He turned to Aunt Z and held up his punch. "Long live the Zantonys!" He took a sip then added, "Aunt Z, I think I'm ready for that ride in your pink hearse."

"Anytime, AJ-kins," Aunt Zsofia chirped.

AJ smiled.

Across the room, in the hearth, Vlad winked and grinned, flashing the gold tooth.

Chapter 32

Two weeks later, Aunt Zsofia invited AJ, his parents, and Emily over for a traditional Hungarian dinner.

The Halloween decorations had been packed away. Mrs. Bones was back in the basement and the Zantony coffin was returned to public storage. The pink hearse was in the shop for a tune-up and Aunt Z had adopted a new puppy from Craggy Cove Critter Rescue. She named him Wolfgang.

Wolfie bounced at AJ's feet as they sat down in the formal dining room. Aunt Zsofia dished out the goulash and passed a basket of her homemade bread.

"How was the Ball?" AJ's dad asked.

"Out of this world!" Aunt Zsofia answered. "It went off without a hitch."

AJ and Emily exchanged glances. Nobody else in Craggy Cove knew the truth about what actually happened on Halloween night. Except Vlad. And he'd never tell.

All through dinner, Aunt Zsofia glowed. Her Monster Ball had been a smashing success. She had raised enough money to pay the yearly taxes on Zala Manor, repaint the mansion's shutters a fresh *Periwinkle Purple,* and repair Serai Zantony's severed headstone. She even splurged and bought a pink wetsuit, flippers, and goggles off eBay.

The handsome vampire from the Monster Troupe, Horace, had invited her to go snorkeling in Craggy Cove Bay next weekend.

After dinner, Aunt Zsofia shared the photos taken the night of the Ball. "AJ, here are the snapshots I took of you and Emily the day you helped me decorate." She handed him a packet of pictures.

AJ flipped through them and stopped dead on the image of him standing on his skateboard in the coffin. A chill shot down his spine. A ghostly apparition hovered near his head just beyond the coffin. AJ gasped. He blinked and looked again.

"What?" Emily whispered. "What is it?"

"I'll show you in the library." With Wolfie at his heels, AJ marched into the library and straight to the painting of the sad boy with the blue eyes. He showed Emily the photo. "See anything... strange?"

Emily's gaze bounced from the photograph, to AJ, to the painting. "Omigosh!"

"It's the same boy," AJ said. "Do you see it? The ghost in this picture looks just like the boy in this painting. I told you this house is haunted."

"Don't start that again."

"Okay. Okay."

Aunt Zsofia's bubbly laughter wafted into the library.

"Hey!" Emily's gaze shifted to the bookcase. "This is our chance to shut the attic window."

"Good idea," AJ said. "But no snooping."

AJ, Emily, and Wolfie stole up the hidden staircase to the attic. As AJ hurried to the window, he spotted a message scrawled in blood on the far wall. He gulped and pointed.

Emily read it aloud. "Beware of the undead, Zantony!"

"Ozor!" AJ cringed. "But…I thought he was gone for good."

Emily crept toward the wall. "It's dried blood. I bet Count Ozor flew back in and left that message before you kicked major vampire butt."

Suddenly Wolfie scampered behind an old steamer trunk and barked.

"What is it, Wolfie?" Emily called.

"Could it be…?" AJ backed toward the door.

Wolfie barked then let out a yelp as he skidded back around the trunk, tumbled across the attic floor, and plowed into AJ.

"AWK!" Vlad appeared on top of the trunk, slashing his blue parrot feather like a pirate sword. "Away, ye maggoty sea mutt!"

"Vlad!" AJ and Emily yelled together. Wolfie let out a little whimper and scuttled behind AJ's legs.

"Ye be needing to teach that mutt a few rules of the pirate code!" Vlad squawked. "So, mateys, did you bring me any scraps from dinner?"

"No, but we can arrange that…if you help us with our science project," Emily said.

"Yeah, we've been thinking that maybe you and a few of your buddies could help us out," AJ said.

"Blast! Science experiment! Look what happened the last time." He pointed to the lumpy scars on his head.

"No, it's nothing like that!" AJ said. "We just want to show how smart you are! We promise, you won't get hurt."

"And what be in it for me, swabbers?" Vlad jabbed his feather at them.

"Name your price," Emily said.

"Hmmm…." Vlad tapped his tail and twisted his whiskers. "Scraps for life—"

"Deal!" AJ said.

"—and a few trips to exotic places!" Vlad sat back on his haunches, folded his arms, and stuck his snout in the air. "But not until I see what ye lads have in mind."

"It's cool, Vlad. I think you'll like it," AJ said.

The following Saturday morning, AJ and Emily arrived at the school cafeteria. A huge banner hung across the wall announcing, "Craggy Cove Middle School Science Fair."

AJ and Emily were the last students to demonstrate their project, a *Rat Water Maze*. Vlad and a few rat pals swam through a multilevel, Plexiglass maze. Vlad propelled himself through the difficult course like an Olympic champion. At the end of the challenge, the rats received a reward of muenster cheese.

Everyone cheered and whistled for the swimming rats. Judges were amazed at how fast the rats found their way through the passages. AJ and Emily were awarded first place.

"Hooray! We're going to the state finals!" Emily jumped up and down.

AJ pumped his fist into the air. "Yessssss!" He let Emily keep the blue ribbon to add to her collection.

After climbing out of the maze and shaking off the water, Vlad winked at AJ and Emily. Then he sniffed the air, scurried down the table leg, and headed for the kitchen. All of the other rats poured onto the floor and followed.

Calvin, Dirk, and Runt jammed out of the cafeteria, screaming and flailing their arms. "Rats! I hate rats!" Calvin screeched as he bumped Dirk and Runt out of the way.

Using hot dogs and a bag of corn chips, AJ lured Vlad and his rat buddies back into a cardboard box for their trip home.

Back at Zala Manor, he and Emily let them out in the basement with the leftover cheese. Vlad's buddies grabbed their share and scattered.

"Wait, Vlad!" AJ called as Vlad started to stuff cheese into his cheeks. "One more question before you go...."

Vlad paused.

"Where is the hidden treasure?" AJ asked.

Vlad's eyes twinkled. He munched on the cheese and smacked his lips, then spat out a pirate ditty:

> *"Ye lads ask where the treasure be,*
> *Yeo-heave-ho and a bottle of rum.*
> *I'll never tell! AWK! Don't ask me!*
> *Har! Har! Har!"*

Coming! Fall 2010!

MONSTER MOON #2:
Secret of Haunted Bog

Fart spray. Check. Whoopee cushion. Check. Itching powder. Check.

AJ invites Emily Peralta and his best friend Freddy "Hangman" Gallows on a trip to old Chinatown. Freddy pulls out his smelliest pranks as he is not about to step aside and let a girl steal his best friend without a fight.

But from the moment they step off the train in Chinatown, Emily becomes the least of their problems. A mysterious fortune-teller warns Freddy of looming danger. A shadowy stranger lurks in the crowded alleyways. Is he following them? Why?

They end up lost in a dark and marshy bog, where they are surrounded by thick fog, creepy sounds, bizarre creatures, and ghostly apparitions. Somebody doesn't want them to escape. But who?

Freddy worries that they might end up at his dad's mortuary lying beneath a white sheet. Why didn't they stay home?

Can AJ and his ZomBuddies work together to come out alive?

Future books in the Monster Moon series:

MONSTER MOON: Parade of Angry Ghosts

It's New Year's and the ZomBuddies volunteer to decorate Craggy Cove's float in the world-famous Pasadena Tournament of Roses Parade. They never expected to find angry ghosts out to ruin the parade. Can the ZomBuddies stop them before the television cameras start rolling?

MONSTER MOON: Lights, Camera, Monsters!

While the ZomBuddies are sightseeing in Hollywood, California, AJ's friend Michael Castro, is discovered by a talent scout for a part in a scary movie. On the set, real monsters lurk among the actors and it is up to the ZomBuddies to re-write the script before someone ends up dead.

MONSTER MOON: The Legend of Monster Island

Slurp. Slurp. Slurp. Something big is clogging the toilets of Craggy Cove and the sewer rats are in danger. In search for answers, the Zombuddies are sucked into sea monster lore. A light rain turns to a monster storm, stranding the ZomBuddies on a small island off the coast of Craggy Cove. The friends take refuge in a cave which turns out to be the nest of a giant sea monster. Can they escape?

MONSTER MOON: A Monster Reunion

I vant my mummy! The Zantonys aren't the only ones headed for an ancestral castle in the secluded mountains of Transylvania for a family reunion. Their ancestors are having a monster gathering of their own, and they are looking forward to welcoming AJ and the ZomBuddies for a time they'll never forget.

MONSTER MOON: House of Creepy Mirrors

I hate clowns! The carnival is coming to Craggy Cove, and the ZomBuddies are the first in line to buy tickets to enter the "House of Creepy Mirrors." A purple-lipped clown is dying to turn their lives inside-out and upside-down. Everybody comes out of the maze except Emily. AJ and his younger cousin, Jasmyn, go back inside to search for her. But all they find is Emily's "I Hate Clowns" baseball cap. AJ summons the ZomBuddies to help find Emily before the carnival packs up and leaves town.

MONSTER MOON: Day of the Dead

Parades, dancing skeletons, and sugar skulls. The ZomBuddies jet to Mexico to celebrate the Day of the Dead with Emily's Mexican father, an archeologist. But the traditional celebrations turn deadly when some of the livestock on Emily's uncle's ranch turn up mutilated. And superstitious ranchers blame the mythical creature El Chupacabra. Can Emily prove there's a logical explanation?

MONSTER MOON: Trapped in Pirate Time

Yeo-heave-ho and a 300-year-old message in a bottle. Emily leads the ZomBuddies as they travel back in time to the days of pillaging pirates. They search for pirate treasure to save present-day Zala Manor from the grips of Mr. Crone, the greedy banker. They find an old ship's compass with clues leading to a treasure map. Vlad, who accompanies them, attempts to change history and prevent the kidnapping that led to his brain transplant. Can the ZomBuddies navigate their way back to the present? Or will they remain forever trapped in pirate time?

Acknowledgements

We would like to thank Stephanie Jefferson for her invaluable contribution to the first draft of this manuscript.

Many thanks for the helpful comments from our first readers: Emily Storey, Jasmyn Jolly, Tali Craig, and Rick Mendoza.

Thanks to the Reading Buddies of Grant and McKinley Elementary schools in Colton, California, for listening to the drafts of this book and for their enthusiastic comments.

This project could never have come to completion without our final readers: Nancy O'Connor and Carol J. Amato. Thanks.

We are grateful to the Riverside critique group for their inspiration and encouragement: Stephanie, Carol, Steve, Beulah, Leah, Sarah, Rilla, Julie, Cindy, Tommy, Marissa, and Nancy.

Monster thanks to Dave Sant for designing our website, www.monstermoonmysteries.com.

Thank you to the restaurants and coffee shops that allow writers to sit for hours and work on their manuscripts. For us, that includes our favorites: Starbucks, Mi Tortilla, Farmer Boys, and Panera Bread.

And we appreciate the hospitality during our stay at the historic Mission Inn in Riverside, California. Thanks to the accommodating staff who took us on a private tour of the catacombs. Not only was it helpful in the writing of this book, but it was great fun!

Of course, we wish to thank all our friends and families for their support and encouragement as we worked on this book. Special thanks to Irene Adame, Pam Elliott, and Geoffrey Sant. Finally, we wish to acknowledge our canine crew, who often sat by our sides as we typed away: Jack and Sally; Callie, Icey, and Thor; Shadow, Maverick, Thorn, and Dude. Woof! Woof!

—LK, KS, and MT

About the Authors

BBH McChiller is the creation of the minds of three authors:

Lynn Kelley worked as a court reporter for 25 years while she and her husband, George, raised their four little monsters. Her story, "The Jobo Tree" won her *Highlights for Children*'s Author of the Month Award. She authored a picture book, *Merry as a Cricket* (WhipperSnapper Books), and is currently working on a young adult novel. She tries to keep her overactive imagination in check and is a big scaredy cat who's afraid to watch horror movies. She lives in Southern California.

Kathryn Sant loves adventure anywhere in the world, and the more off the beaten path, the better. Over the years she has encountered bats in caves, alligators in swamps, wolves and bears in Alaska, parrots and macaws in the jungle, sidewinders in the sand dunes, llamas in the Andes mountains, and caribou in the Arctic, but never any monsters. On a trip to Urquhart, Scotland, she tried to spot the Loch Ness Monster, but failed to see anything except the other side of the lake. Of all the monsters, she would most like to meet the Yeti or the Ogopogo. Most of the time she lives peacefully in Southern California with her three dogs, reading....sometimes about monsters.

Maria Toth lives in Southern California with her husband and their two spoiled dogs, Jack and Sally. Her favorite holiday is Halloween. She enjoys haunting book stores in search of ghostly tales to share with her Reading Buddies at local schools. On any given day, you may find her reading epitaphs at historic graveyards. And she is not afraid of monsters, so long as they stay within the realms of her imagination. But just in case, she always keeps a bottle of Monster Spray nearby.

```
+
MCCHI

McChiller, BBH.
Curse at Zala Manor
Robinson JUV CIRC
04/10
```